One Take Jake

Jay Lang

Print ISBNs
Amazon print 9780228626381
Ingram Spark 9780228626398
Barnes & Noble 9780228626404

BWL Publis...

Books we love to write ...
Authors around the world.

http://bwlpublishing.ca

Acknowledgements

Special thanks to Joe Lynn Turner, and Joel Hoekstra, Chris Caffery, Scot Bihlman, Rob Lamothe, Lance Campbell, Darren Moore, Roxanne, Soren Andersen, and many more. I appreciate all of your participation and support.

And to my jewel, Jules, who edits persistently to make my work shine.

Celebrity Endorsements

One Take Jake is a heroic tale that ends in tragedy.

It is said that tragedy is the imitation of a noble and complete action which through compassion and fear produces purification of the passions.

Our human emotions such as anger, fear, betrayal, remorse, loss, love, etc. can shut down our rational and logical thought process and create a mindset of confusion and lack of judgment.

As passion overwhelms the main character,

Our noble hero is filled with anger and revenge and makes some seriously bad decisions and ends up being a sacrificial lamb.

I believe life is a decision and all situations and outcomes are the end result of those decisions. Which in turn creates the sum total of our lives.

It defines our habits and actions, and eventually, our character and our character ultimately determines our fate.

One Take Jake could be anybody's story.

Acting out of non-selfish intentions, Lance is caught in a web of human intervention and emotion, and by making some foolish decisions, he seals his fate.

What began as a noble cause ends in a tragic account of arguably an unjust punishment.

The ancient stoics believed in Amor Fati, a Latin phrase that means, love one's fate. Good or bad we must embrace it and suffer the consequences of our actions.

Read this fascinating story and reserve judgment for yourself. Only you can make that decision. **Joe Lynn Turner**

"Hollywood's trend of depicting women in warrior and super-heroine roles in recent years is a great thing to see, as it celebrates the strength and empowerment of women; a tenet most societies badly need to embrace. But it also belies a more fundamental and much older undercurrent: Women everywhere are at risk of predation, to some degree, at all times.

The entertainment industry's waters are filthy with sharks—from con artists to legal thieves to sexual predators—all swimming around the less-legit outskirts, looking for the next stars-in-the-eyes hopeful to snare. And some of this happens in the music industry."

- **Byron Fry**, **composer/producer/studio musician** byronfry.com

"A lot of people are obsessed with celebrities, and being around an admired music artist can certainly be alluring and exciting. The reality is that many in the music industry are in it because they can express themselves in a way that they are unable to in real life. This ability to connect with people, with their music or message, can put them in a position of power.

Unfortunately, some are bad, and have bad intentions and a willingness to abuse this power and take advantage of music fans. Some are sexual predators who have no respect for others.

Those of us who are in it for the music and expressing ourselves are victims too because it makes us all look bad. Hopefully, bringing these issues to light will lead to improvement for all involved in this inspiring art form."

- **Mikey Capone**, **producer/guitarist/songwriter - Sons of Toil** sonsoftoil.com

"I can say I've come across some kind souls in the music world over my career. However, in my 45 years in the Business of Music, I've also experienced all kinds of manipulation and suppression that apparently comes with the territory. Cheers to those who Fight the Good fight."

- Darby Mills, vocalist (The Queen of Scream) - Headpins, Darby Mills Project darbymills.com

"Music is the great equalizer. It does not recognize gender, bias, or anything else for that matter. From my perspective, music is an expression of the soul. It is a sharing of thoughts, feelings, and intentions, and for some, it is an ongoing dialogue, a conversation between musicians - often simultaneously, at several different levels of communication. Where does anything other than a pure expression of an art form make the 'jump' to the vital topics peeled back and revealed, as Jay has done in this much-needed perspective?"

- Dan Bodanis, studio drummer/big band leader - Dan Bodanis Big Band dbbb.ca

"Being a musician and producer, I've also seen and experienced this type of disturbing problem with sexual predators trying to manipulate others in the music business. This is a very important topic drawing attention and starting a conversation about these individuals still out there causing mental and physical abuse. The music industry is full of respectable artists and executives (record labels and managers) who have dedicated most of their lives to building fanbases and a career. In this modern day, there is no room or tolerance for abusive people that prey on both young and older women and men!"

- Johnny Gasparic, producer/engineer/musician - The Robert Gosse Band, The Poverty Plainsmen mccrecording.com

"Abusive behaviour in any industry is unacceptable, especially in the entertainment industry which is already guilty of exploitation of women and young girls. Thank you for bringing attention to this issue."

- *Danny Deane, singer/producer/engineer - Best of Both Worlds artfarm.ca*

"It's extremely sad that some people in the limelight would take advantage of that role. To any musicians, industry people, producers, or agents: Be the person you want the world to believe you are."

- *Dan Todd, drummer - FourOneSix, Platinum Blonde, Alannah Myles, FLUDD, Jimi Jamison, Honeymoon Suite IG: @drummerdantodd FB: Dan Todd Fan page*

"I'm honored to be included in Jay's story and to back her up in bringing to light what we all know happens in our field. She has the voice and the medium to reach more people and hopefully inspire a change."

- *Reggie Hache-bassist, producer/session Musician Reggiehache.com*

"As far as deviants in the industry, I've seen them on TV. But I don't know any of them personally. I couldn't be friends with deviants like that. Personally, I haven't come across anything like that. I mean, as a traveling musician when you're young yeah, you sleep with people, but it was all consensual. I'm looking forward to reading this book."

- Darren Smith, vocalist - Harem Scarem, Red Dragon Cartel haremscarem.net

"The music industry is full of respectable artists who have dedicated their lives to honing their skills and building fanbases. There is no room and no tolerance for abusive deviants that prey on young women. This is completely unacceptable to us artists who are just trying to create, inspire and bring a sense of peace, love, and hope to our audiences."

- Michael Mezzina, producer/composer - Fragile Sky IG: @fragileskyrock

"As a professional musician who has worked in the entertainment business for over 40 years, it's refreshing to see an author like Jay Lang present the very real and very dark reality of sexual abuse that occurs in the industry. Hopefully shedding light on this hushed evil will motivate and inspire people to take action and speak out against predators."

- **Lance Chalmers, drummer/session musician - Trooper, Sweeney Todd sabian.com/artist/lance-chalmers**

"Being in the music industry for almost 30 years, I've heard about predatory behaviour occurring. Thankfully, I've never experienced anything personally. The musicians I've surrounded myself with have always been professional and primarily focused on their work."

- **Ute Ehrenberg, singer/manager/producer nedyjcross.com**

"The music business is a highly dynamic industry with many peaks and valleys. As a recording artist and touring musician, I have unfortunately heard about this predatorily dynamic with musicians who use their status to take advantage of women. This behaviour has tainted our industry and perpetuates a dynamic that is unacceptable and damages the upstanding people who do it for the art."

-Scot Little Bihlman, drummer/singer/multi-instrumentalist - Grinder Blues, John Fogerty, Jelly Roll scotbihlman.com

"The sexual exploitation of young women is ubiquitous in the music business. It's disturbing how some people of notoriety choose to use their influence. Keep shining your light, Jay."

- Darcy D, Virtual Voice Coach/artist developer/vocalist – Prism virtualvoice.coach

"It's always a shame when good people let their egos do stupid thoughtless things that hurt others and honestly shame us all, as an educated race of people. This is in all walks of life, not just the entertainment industry. I don't understand how some people don't have the ability to stop and think for one second about how an act, which doesn't feel right to begin with, is going to affect others and ultimately themselves. The mass majority of us certainly don't condone destructive behaviour, we also don't allow it within our purview. As individuals we recognize it as a problem and crime. However, our system supports the opinions and actions of elitists, enforced by a corrupt legal and political system. It's sad."

- **Darren Moore, singer/musician/producer - Snake Oil snakeoilrock.com**

Table of Contents

Chapter 1

The jet lag clings to me like a bad hangover after a grueling thirteen-plus hour flight from Zurich to Vancouver. It's hard to believe I was sitting in a top-of-the-line studio just a day and a half ago with three other great players. Granted, we're only studio musicians, and although we're paid well, our prominence diminishes after we pack up our instruments and leave the building.

I look over the bouquet of fresh pink flowers perfectly positioned at the centre of the shiny wooden coffin. A half-dozen older women with wide-brimmed hats and black Coco Chanel dresses have their heads down, sobbing, or should I say performance-sobbing. Although West Van boasts many down-to-earth folks, these six are not among them. My mother joined a social club years ago, where she met this group of pariahs. They are widows, or their husbands replaced them with younger versions. The only reason they've slithered down from their ivory towers today is to gain popularity by feigning sympathy for my mother. If there were an authentic bone in any of them, they would've supported my mother when she lost Dad seven years ago. Still, I guess here, at a funeral, they're more likely to be seen by members of the community and receive accolades for their visible compassion. It makes me sick.

I feel like shouting at them to get the fuck away from us. They have no business here. It's not like they gave two shits about me or my sister, and to see them now giving top performances is an insult.

I look down at my mom, standing beside me. Her once shapely frame has been eaten away by grief and guilt. If only she told me what was happening with Hannah, I could've hopped the next plane home and been here to protect my kid sister. After all, I was the closest person to her. She confided in me and trusted me more than any other person, and even though she was seven years my junior— she at twenty and me almost twenty-eight— we were friends, best friends, at least until a few months ago when her emails abruptly stopped. I should've clued in that something sinister was going on then.

"Drugs" was my mother 's only word when I asked how Hannah died. I spent the entire flight slamming back rye and cokes to numb the pain—it didn't work. Stewed in watered-down booze, I stumbled off the plane, grabbed a cab to the house, and sat silently in my old room, staring out the window.

She was an A student and always followed the rules. She was, by all accounts, a textbook definition of the word *nerd*—all except for her looks. Long golden hair and flawless skin, and she developed early, making me amp up my already overprotectiveness over her. My friends used to jerk my chain and make offhanded comments about Hannah's killer body. Usually, their banter earned them a hard shot on the arm or a swack up the back of the head, but I knew they were only half joking. I could tell by the way men looked at her that my baby sister had unknowingly developed into a stunning young woman—all compressed into a petite five-foot-three frame.

I can't help but suspect that her looks attracted the attention of an unsavory predator that lured her away. Whoever pulled her into darkness and got her hooked on the drugs that killed her, I will find them.

My mother grabs my arm. "I think I'd like to leave now."

I nod, then put my hand over hers and slowly walk her to the car.

"It was a nice service. Don't you think, Lance?"

"It was beautiful, Mom."

"I think Hannah would've loved the pink carnations." She sniffs back tears. "They were her favourite flower."

"They were perfect."

With only a few feet to go before we make it to Dad's old Mercedes, two women approach us from behind. "Anne," one of the women calls out.

Reluctantly I turn, Mom still attached to my arm.

The two old birds are regulars at my mother's bridge group. Both have red eyes and wadded-up tissues in their hands.

"Hello. Thank you so much for coming," Mom says, letting go of my arm.

As the ladies speak with my mother, I focus on everyone who attended the funeral. About fifty in total, if I had to guess. Most I see are older and have a connection to my mom, not Hannah.

That is until I glimpse a girl in the distance, walking away. She has multi-coloured hair and seems headed for the parking lot at the far end of the graveyard.

I quickly excuse myself from the trio, telling my mother I'll be right back. I then briskly walk in the direction of the girl—if this person knew Hannah, maybe they can give me some insight into the life she was living, and who she was with before she died.

As the girl steps off the neatly manicured grass and onto the pavement, I call out to her, "Hey. Excuse me." My voice is a little louder than intended.

She turns, and I'm surprised when I recognize her as one of the kids who hung out with Hannah after school. She looks different now. Harder. Like all the innocence and youth have been prematurely drained from her.

"Jenny. Is that you?"

"I was wondering if you'd make it back for the funeral." Her voice is raspy and cold.

"Yeah. I haven't been back long. How are you?"

She shakes her head. "Better than Hannah, that's for sure."

"Look, Jenny. I've been away for a while—a full year. Apparently, Hannah was doing drugs, and she OD'd. You know anything about that?"

Like a flipped switch, Jenny suddenly gets a dark look. "No. I wasn't her keeper."

"I just thought since you guys were such good friends, you might know what she was up to—"

"Well, I don't. And I'm in a hurry, so I should probably get going." She reaches into her pocket and pulls out a set of keys. "It was nice to see you again, Lance. And I'm sorry about your sister."

I watch as she gets into a 70's model Ford Pinto, the only car that earned its own trademark song, "Disco Inferno" by the Tramps, due to a faulty design in the rear end that, when bumped, even a little, tended to burst into flames.

Walking back toward my mother and her friends, I remember more about Jenny. She would often come to the house and do homework with Hannah. When I walked past her room, their loud voices would quickly lower to whispers. They were close, close enough that one summer, Jenny came with us on a family vacation to Kelowna.

Remembering this and how dismissive Jenny was to me now, I'm positive she knows a hell of a lot more about what happened to my sister than she's telling. For the time being, she's on my radar and the only lead I have.

* * *

After getting Mom home and maneuvering my way around countless bouquets set unintentionally in the hallway, I make a pot of tea while Mom slumps down in my father's worn-out La-Z-Boy. After the kettle whistles, I throw a bag into a cup, add two sugars, and carry the hot drink into the living room.

"Here, Mom." I set the tea on the stand beside her.

She waves her hand dismissively. "No. I need something stronger. There's a bottle of vodka in the freezer."

"Vodka?" I glance up at the clock. "It's only 10 AM."

"I didn't ask for your judgment, son. I asked for the vodka. And just to be clear, you weren't the one who buried a child today, so your rules don't apply."

"I don't have rules, Mom. I'm just concerned, is all."

Seeing her this rattled and weak, I let the subject slide for now, reluctantly walking to the freezer to retrieve the bottle. Once back in the living room, I sit on the sofa and watch my mother's shaking hands as she pours her drink. "Are you okay?" I prepare myself for another defensive outburst.

"Well, I'm here. That's a lot more than I can say for my daughter."

"I know. It's been so hard for you. I just wish you would've told me what was going on. I would've been here."

"I didn't want to worry you. Plus, things were already spinning out of control with your sister. I didn't need you showing up and causing trouble on top of it all."

"I wouldn't have caused trouble, Mom. But I could've supported you and talked some sense into Hannah."

She takes a big drink. "So, it's my fault? Is that what you're saying?"

I stare at her. "What are you talking about? I don't blame you at all."

"You're saying I never called so that you could've saved Hannah's life. So, by the lack of action on my part, your sister died."

The woman sitting across from me is not my mother. Or at least, she's not the mother that raised me. She looks similar, though a hell of a lot thinner and weaker. But it's more so the attitude. My mother was soft-spoken and gentle by nature, unlike the bitter woman taking gulps of vodka sitting across from me now.

23

For the next few minutes, I persuade her that she's got me all wrong, then reassure her that she's not being blamed, nor should she carry the burden of Hannah's death. My efforts seem to pay off, or maybe it's just the effects of the vodka because my mother's sternness eventually eases, her voice lowers, and her waifish body slumps deeper into the chair.

She closes her eyes for a brief moment, and a large teardrop escapes from the corner of her eye and rolls over her pointy cheekbone. "She was the most wonderful child." She turns her attention to a family picture on the wall. "She always listened and never stepped over the line. And her heart...have you ever met a human being with such a beautiful heart?"

"No, Mom. Never. And I don't imagine I ever will again."

My mother turns her eyes to mine. "Then how come you haven't cried yet?"

"I don't know. I guess that deep down, I can't really believe it's true. It's hard to believe Hannah would just turn to drugs all on her own."

She studies my face for a few moments. "You're not planning on causing any trouble, are you?"

"Don't be silly, Mom. What kind of trouble could I possibly cause?"

"That's good, son." She sounds unconvinced. "I once read a line. *An eye for an eye leaves the whole world blind.* Sounded like good sense to me."

I nod to appease her.

"You were never much of a crier, now that I think about it. Even after your father died. Sure, it slowed you down for a while, and you were quieter, but no tears. It's the oddest thing, really. I mean, a child loses a parent and doesn't let go of one tear. Maybe I should've taken you to a doctor or something, but I was too wrapped up in my own grief at the time."

"I'm not insensitive if that's what you're suggesting. I grieve in my own way, that's all."

She laughs. "You were so mad at your dad when he sat you down and told you he had cancer. He thought you were going to take a swing at him. It definitely wasn't the reaction any of us expected."

"That's me. Your son, the freak."

She smiles. "No, Lance. That's the confusing part. You're the kindest soul. But you tend to go a bit off the deep end when something unjust happens. Anger has always been your go-to emotion."

"Maybe you should try to eat something." I'm eager to change the subject. Besides, straight vodka on an empty stomach will burn holes through her.

"I'll eat later. For now, I just want to go to my room and lie down."

Now that she's out of her reactive mood, I realize it's a safer time to ask about

Hannah. "Just to give me closure, can you tell me what happened over the last while with Hannah? Just a bit?"

She shrugs. "It all happened so fast, like a freak accident or a flash storm. Hannah was as she always was, working every day at Starbucks and coming straight home. She was never late for dinner and always told me where she was going on the weekends. I never had much to be concerned about with that girl."

"Until when?"

Mom takes another gulp from her glass. "The concert. It was afterward that things changed."

"What concert?"

"One of those rock bands."

"That's strange. Why would Hannah go to a rock concert? She hates concerts."

My mother squints as if she's trying to remember. "Her friend was over for dinner and mentioned she'd gotten free tickets to see a group playing at a club downtown."

"Which friend had the tickets?"

"Jenny."

I take a deep, silent breath, then keep probing. "Do you remember the name of the band?"

"No. It was a silly name. I remember laughing when I heard it out loud."

"What happened after Hannah and Jenny went to the concert?"

"She changed just like that. Overnight."

"How?"

"The first thing I noticed was the amount of time she spent holed up in her room with her door shut. We never shut our doors before, so I found it quite odd. But it wasn't only that. About a week after the concert, she told me the Starbucks she worked at was closing. I didn't know it was a lie until the day I went to the mall to get my watch fixed."

"The Starbucks was still open?"

She nods. "I confronted her when I got home, and she became furious. She screamed and hollered at me to mind my own business. She even threw the little porcelain ballerina at the wall and broke it. The one your father gave me."

It's so strange to hear her speak about my meek-mannered sister like this. "Go on, Mom."

"Things went from bad to worse after that. She would stay out all night and come home just long enough to have a shower and grab something to eat. And every time I tried to ask her what she was up to, a big fight broke out. I was losing my sweet child and could do nothing about it." Tears run down her cheeks, and she takes another swig of vodka. "I'm tired, Lance. I'm too tired to talk anymore."

Mom went to bed, taking her half glass of vodka with her.

I can't believe everything that happened while I was gone or what's happening now that I'm back. It's like I've been transported into a parallel universe where everything I know is now the complete opposite. In this dark and strange world, my innocent and beautiful baby sister was a drug addict, and my mother, a woman that lived her life by example, now lies emaciated and drunk in the other room, rendered down to a walking skeleton. I don't know this world. And I sure as hell don't recognize these people as my family.

I force in a deep breath and close my eyes. As the air escapes my lungs, I feel a deep trembling throughout my body.

I've got to get out of here. Maybe go for a walk around the neighbourhood to clear my head. But first, while she's hibernating in her room, I've got to go through the cupboards and the trash. I need to know just how bad her drinking has gotten.

When I left for Europe just over a year ago, my mother didn't drink a drop. Even while growing up, it was rare someone could talk her into indulging in a glass of wine or even a splash of champagne on New Year's. But the way she was swilling back the vodka this morning, her face barely changing with every gulp, I suspect she's been self-medicating to chase away the pain she's been feeling over Hannah.

Attempting not to make too much noise, I carefully open the cupboard under the sink. When I crouch to take a thorough look, all I see is a bucket full of cleaning sponges, three or four bottles of Windex, and other forms of scrubbing detergents.

Under the drainpipe is the small rectangular trash bin that's always been there. I tip it toward me, but other than a Mr. Big wrapper, it's pretty much empty.

I continue my search, first above the fridge and then in the higher shelves of the cabinets, but there's no trace of alcohol. The closest thing I find is an old bottle of pure vanilla, but by the look of the crusty lid, it hasn't been opened since probably before I left.

I'm just about to admit I may have guessed wrong about her boozing when my eyes hit the far side of the kitchen, where the garage door is.

I wonder.

The door handle creaks loudly, causing me to freeze and listen for the sound of Mom racing down the steps to bust me, but thankfully the house is still dead quiet. I turn the knob slowly until the latch clicks, then gently open the door and walk into the narrow one-car garage that quickly became a storage room over the past year.

Everything is pretty much the same as when I was last in here: boxes piled up in the corners, and old trunks, lamps, and rejected appliances take up the majority of space. I walk over to a couple of new recycling bins sitting in the corner under long, dusty spiderwebs.

The size of the bins far exceeds the output of waste my mother would go through over an entire year. A sick feeling bubbles in the pit of my gut as I lift the lid of the first bin.

A hot waft of stale booze escapes. I look down in amazement at the gathering of empty bottles, all different kinds—gin, whiskey, ciders, and, of course, vodka.

As I stand with my mouth open, my fingers weaken, and the lid slips from my grasp and slams shut. Still in a semi-zombie state of shock, I lift the cover of the second bin only slightly. Sure enough, the first thing I see is the reflection of the garage light on countless different bottles. I slam down the top and close my eyes.

This is fantastic, Mom. I come home after working away for a year, just in time to see my kid sister lowered into a 3 x 8-foot grave. And, as if that's not enough to tip me over the edge, I now find out that my once-strong mother has swum to the bottom of a booze bottle. I don't know what's hitting me harder—the horror that you hid this from me or the sheer amazement that you're still alive.

Realizing that my processing and coping skills are waning quickly, I head back into the house, grab my phone, and head out.

* * *

The familiar odour of freshly mowed lawns rides on the air as I walk down the sidewalk and cross the road to the old park. I remember taking Hannah here when she was little, about five or six. Back then, there were far more kids than there were things to play on, so the line-ups were long. Hannah, being the painfully shy child she was, made me stand with her among all the other impatient kids. As long and tedious the task was then, I'd give anything to relive even one of those times with her now.

Children's laughter and joyful summertime noises enter my ears only briefly before they get drowned out by the dark chaos churning in my mind. I spot a vacant bench not far from the sea walk at the edge of the playground and sit. The day started out clear and sunny, but as I gaze over the water at the rolling, angry clouds and smell the sudden acrid odour of ozone in the air, I know we are in for a storm at some point tonight.

I watch the ebb and flow of the tide as it pushes the waves ashore, and my mind flashes back to the cemetery, to when I was standing only feet away from where my sweet baby sister lay in her coffin.

A part of me wanted to leap forward and pull the lid open to see Hannah one last time. From what my mother muttered to me when I first arrived at the house, I learned the hospital morgue had asked Mom if she wanted to view Hannah's body before it was transported to the funeral home. Mom declined, but I wouldn't have. It would have helped me to see her, how she looked when she drew her last breath, and if she had any marks signifying abuse or mistreatment. Now, I'm left to solve a huge puzzle without a single piece.

Except for Jenny. She's my solitary path into what was going on in Hannah's life. Even though Jenny doesn't know it, she'll tell me everything she knows.

When the first spit of rain hits, I take a deep breath and slowly stand. I don't want to go back to the house. All that awaits me there is my alcohol-saturated mother. There's another clusterfuck I have to deal with—figuring out how to talk some sense into her and convincing her to seek professional help. I know two things about my mother: she won't change her mind once she decides something, and she hates people sticking their noses into personal business.

Alcoholism is definitely personal business.

I've got my work cut out for me.

Chapter 2

I take the long way home, around the schoolyard where I attended junior high and through the woods that lead to a street two down from ours. As I walk, I reflect on the earlier conversation I had with Mom. Her talking about how I can't, or don't, show emotion.

She's wrong, of course. I clearly remember numerous times as a child when I would hurt myself or when I was very frustrated, and the tears would flow easily. The last time I remember sobbing was at the hospital, the day my father passed away.

He had just visited with my mother and asked to speak with me alone. For some reason, I was nervous to go into his room. I'd never had anyone close to me die before, and the very thought was too much to bear. I remember walking in and seeing him lying in the bed with the metal railings up. He was staring at the ceiling, a two-pronged air hose plugged into his nose.

When he sensed me there, he slowly pulled the hose away from his face. "Come here, Lance."

I walked up to the bed and gripped the cold sidebars. "I'm here, Dad."

"I need you to be the man of the house. Promise me that you'll protect your mother and sister. Can you do that?"

"Of course. I promise I'll do my best."

My father coughed and shook his head. "No. Don't do your best. Be there, and be a man. Make sure nothing happens to them."

I gave him my word. And considering what became of both Hannah and my mother, I couldn't have fucked up more. If there is a heaven, and my father is there, he'll be looking down with sheer disgust right now.

If I had honoured my word to him and hadn't gone to Europe, maybe Hannah and Mom would be okay. But my selfishness won out. When I got the call to travel abroad and collaborate with top musicians, I jumped at the chance—a decision I will regret for the rest of my life.

* * *

I beeline to Mom's room as soon as I enter the house. Her curled body is facing the window with her back to me.

For a second, adrenaline spikes—what if she threw up and choked, or her liver gave out? I'm about to cross the floor when I see her rib cage slightly expand and contract. She's still alive. I grab the handle and slowly back out of the room, closing the door softly.

I'm walking down the carpeted steps to the kitchen when I hear the phone ringing in the front room. Not wanting the sound to wake my mother, I dart into the room and answer on the second ring. "Hello?" I keep my voice quiet.

"Hi. I'm looking for Lance."

I recognize the voice immediately. It's Reggie, my old bass player from Gravity, a 70's cover band we were in together. He's a top-level player with talent that could've easily surpassed my achievements. The only problem was his girlfriend—a real control freak with a tight grip on him. When I left for Europe, I wanted him to come with me. He would've made a lot of connections and money playing on albums and collaborating, but his she-devil had faked a pregnancy, and Reggie, being the stand-up guy he is, opted to stay behind. Only a few months later, the girl came clean and left him to shack up with another musician. The last I heard, Reg worked at a 9-5 warehouse job, creating videos in his spare time and going to as many concerts as possible.

"What's up, Reg?"

"Hey, man. I thought that was you, but your sultry whisper threw me off for a moment. I didn't know if I had accidentally called a dating line or if your mom had laryngitis."

I chuckle and tell him that I can't make a lot of noise because of my mother sleeping. "How did you know I'd be here?"

"I saw Hannah's obit in the paper. I'm really sorry, man. She was a great kid."

"Yeah. It's pretty unbelievable."

"How long you in town for?"

"Not sure. Probably indefinitely. I need to help my mom out."

"Understood. Hey, I'm actually not far from you right now. I just finished shopping at the mall. You feel like coming out for a drink? I can be there in ten minutes if you're up for it. Unless, of course, you're expecting people for the wake?"

"Nah. We opted out of a gathering after the funeral. Neither one of us wanted to deal with that."

"Then maybe getting out for a while is just what you need."

"Yeah. All right, man. Swing by my place, and I'll meet you outside."

I find a piece of paper and a pen to write a quick note for Mom, telling her I'll be back shortly. After setting the note on the counter, I finger-comb my hair in the hallway mirror before quietly heading out the front door.

Making her way down the driveway is Kimberly, our next-door neighbour. She's carrying a baking dish. When she sees me, the sides of her mouth drop.

"Hi there." I do my best to sound upbeat. "How are you?" By the sad look on her face, she's obviously coming to give her condolences. I'm not in the mood for any more sadness.

"Lance. I thought I saw you walking up the street a little while ago. I recognized your long brown hair. I'm so glad you're back. Your mom really needs you. That poor woman has gone through hell."

"Yeah. I know. But don't worry. I'm home now."

Kim's eyes meet mine, and I see tears well up. "I'm so sorry about Hannah. She was such a lovely girl. I just couldn't believe she went off the rails as she did. She didn't seem the type."

I nod, not knowing what to say.

"I brought over some casserole. I'm sure neither of you feels much like cooking right now."

"That was very sweet of you." I take the dish. "I'll pop it in the fridge before leaving. A friend is picking me up—I have to do a few errands while Mom is asleep."

I can tell by Kim's perplexed expression that she's surprised I'm leaving my mother alone so soon after the funeral. "Oh. I see. Well, please tell her I send my best wishes, and I'll stop over tomorrow sometime to check in on her."

Just then, Reggie's blue '72 Lemans pulls up. It's rumbling so loud that Kim and I couldn't continue our conversation if we wanted to, and I don't. I give Reggie a quick wave, smile at Kim, then head back into the house to put the casserole away. When I come back outside, Kim is walking past Reggie's car with her hands over her ears.

I open the door and slide into the car. Reg looks much the same with buzzed short hair, and like he's taken care of himself. I give my old pal a playful punch on the arm. He smiles and nods, and we head down the road.

* * *

Lulu's was arguably the best place to play in the Lower Mainland. On Friday and Saturday nights, line-ups always stretched halfway down the block. The manager, Murph, loved his job and treated us musicians with kindness and respect. He even threw in free appys at the end of the night.

He was a salt-of-the-earth guy but sadly retired. Now, Lulu's has a new manager who looks to be in his early twenties. Instead of hiring kick-ass bands, he opts for DJs who blast shitty contemporary music—a sign of the times. So many great venues in Vancouver have gone the same route. It's cheaper, but a bad decision, if you ask me. All you have to do is compare crowd attendance from when they had live bands to now when all they play is canned music.

Not much we can do to change it. Just have to wait for the pendulum to swing back the other way, I guess.

Reggie and I sit at the bar and order two beers. I quickly beat Reg to the chase and cover the bill.

"Wow." Reggie eyes the place. "This place has gone downhill fast. It's too bad. Lulu's was rockin' back in the day."

"Yeah. When Murph left, he took all the good things about this place with him."

I glance around at the bar as we take the first sips of our drinks. The only people in here besides us are four guys playing pool and a table of half a dozen college types. Reg asks the barman if it's always this dead in here. The man looks down at his watch and tells us that in fifteen minutes, people should start pouring in for lunch. "It's cheap appys day."

When the bartender walks away, Reg turns his chair to face me. "You doing okay, Lance? I can't imagine what you must be going through right now."

I nod and take a drink. "It's weird, man. Since I got back, it feels like I got thrust into the Twilight Zone. Nothing feels real."

"How's your mom holding up?"

I shrug. "Mom's pickled her emotions so much that, other than the odd coherent sentence, she's kind of slipped into zombie mode."

"She's drinking a lot?"

"I'd say so. But I don't want to talk about all of that. I swear, my head's going to explode." I quickly change the subject. "Tell me what you've been up to lately. Have you been playing at all?"

"Where?" Reggie laughs. "There's barely anywhere to play anymore."

"Yeah. I guess we were lucky to be a part of things when they were good, huh?"

Reggie nods. "What about you? How was Europe?"

"It was great. People over there actually appreciate live music, not the canned DJ shit they play here."

"Did you see any good shows when you weren't working in the studio?"

"Yeah. It was crazy. I've seen everyone worth seeing. Just a couple of weeks ago, a few guys from the studio and I saw a super group with all the best North American players. Chris Caffery was on lead—he ripped it up so much, I thought his guitar was gonna catch fire."

"Yeah, I've seen him play on YouTube. Unreal. He plays this amazing flying V that I'd love to get my hands on."

"I'm telling you, there's nothin' but killer shows over there. It's endless. And the huge concerts they have are crazy. A sea of people shows up for every show."

Reggie sighs. "Why do I feel depressed all of a sudden?"

I laugh and elbow him. "Why don't you go to Europe?"

"Yeah, easy for you to say, One Take Jake."

"Don't be stupid. You're an ace player, and I know a lot of great people who'd love to have you do some studio work. I'd definitely put in a good word for you."

"Thanks, man. But I'll need a good demo first, and I just haven't had the time lately. I'm at work every day. When I'm not, I'm so dog tired that I can barely muster the energy to do my laundry."

I'm just about to respond when I see four strange-looking guys walk in. They're dressed head-to-toe in black, with dyed black hair and heavy silver jewellery.

We watch as they make their way to a large corner table. Reggie chuckles. "What the hell was that? Is there a goth convention going on?"

I shake my head. "I don't know, man. But they do look a little ghoulish."

When we finish our drinks, Reggie motions to the bartender and orders two more. While we're waiting, I head to the john, walking past the dark crew in the corner. I shake my head. *Man, Lulu's sure has changed since I used to hang out here.*

When I finish in the bathroom, I'm walking back to the bar when I see a group of young women come in. Immediately, I recognize one of them as Hannah's friend, Jenny. Suddenly, all other thoughts leave my mind.

It's fate that she's here at the same time as me. I've got to wait for the first opportunity to corner her and probe more information about my sister.

I pull some money from my pocket and set it on the counter as the bartender approaches with the beer, then position myself on the stool so my back faces Jenny. I don't want her to spot me. Not yet.

For the next fifteen minutes, Reg talks about some of the bands he's been watching on YouTube. "There's this band out of Oregon called Mad World. You've got to check them out. The drummer and bass player are the tightest rhythm section I've heard in ages. Their names are Kevin and Bruce McKern—brothers, I think. You should check them out."

"I will. Thanks for the heads up." I watch Jenny in the mirror behind the bar.

A few minutes later, she gets up and heads toward the washrooms. Halfway there, she stops, abruptly turns, and heads back to her table. Once there, she leans over and whispers something to her friends, then grabs her purse.

Why is she acting so strange? I'm sure it wasn't me that scared her off—she didn't look toward the bar once. Whatever has ruffled her feathers, I can tell she's getting ready to leave. So as much as getting caught up with Reg has been great, I've got to think of a way to cut our visit short.

Jenny heads quickly toward the entrance. Shit. I have to catch her before she disappears again.

"Hey, Reg. My day is catching up to me. I think I'm going to split and head back to the house."

Reg looks at me, a bit surprised. "Oh. Okay. I understand. You're dealing with a lot right now. Let's finish our beers, and I'll give you a ride back."

"Nah. You sit and drink your beer. I'm just going to grab a cab." I tell him to reach out in the next while, and we'll plan to hang out again. I pat him on the shoulder, then head out to catch Jenny.

The sun is blinding after sitting in the dim bar. I squint as I scan up and down the street—I can't spot Jenny's colourful hair anywhere. A wave of defeat rushes over me. Shit. She was so close. Now, there's no telling when I might run into her again. If ever.

I start on the long walk home. A part of me wants to go back into the bar to ask Reg for a ride, but I'd feel bad doing it after cutting our visit short. As I walk up the street, I watch oncoming traffic for any sign of a taxi.

When I approach an intersection and casually glance around, I see Jenny's shit box Pinto idling at the lights.

Her attention is on her phone, which is resting in her lap. Now's my chance.

I dash to the car and try the passenger door, praying it's not locked—it isn't. I quickly slide in, sitting on her purse. I meet her gaze. Her mouth is open in utter shock.

"What are you doing? Get the hell out of my car."

"Calm down, Jenny. I just want to talk for a couple of minutes. Then I'll get out."

The driver behind us honks as the light turns green. When Jenny grabs the wheel, I notice that her hands are shaking. "You can't just jump into my car. What are you, some sick stalker?" We pull through the intersection.

"Don't flatter yourself, girl. You're not my type. And you know exactly what I want to talk about."

"You want to visit the cop shop right now? Cuz that's where I'm driving if you don't get the fuck out."

"What happened to Hannah after the concert?"

Jenny's eyes widen. "I...I have no idea what the hell you're talking about." She's scanning the traffic as she drives.

"Talk to me, Jenny. I already know you were the one who took her. It was after that concert her life spun out of control. So, what the hell happened?"

"I told you already. I have no idea what happened with Hannah. One minute she was fine, and the next, she wasn't." Anger is overtaking the fear now.

I sniff a laugh without humour. "Okay. Pull over and let me out."

The stress lines on her face relax. "Okay. Good. You crazy ass."

We drive until she spots a large, empty parking lot, where she pulls in and stops the car. She stares hard out the windshield. "Goodbye, Lance."

I quickly reach over and twist the key out of the ignition. Jenny tries to stop me, but I'm already leaning back, her keys out of reach, tight in my fist. "Oh no. I guess you'd better start talking if you want to get out of here."

"Give them back, asshole, or I swear I'll—"

"You'll what? Scream for help? Go for it." I level my gaze. "If the cops show up, I'll tell them I saw you take a handful of pills. No cop's going to arrest me for taking car keys from an impaired driver."

"I haven't taken any pills."

"The cops won't know that. They'll send you to the hospital to have your stomach pumped, and I assure you, it won't be fun. So, I suggest you take a second, calm the hell down, then open your mouth and start answering my questions."

Jenny raises her fists and bangs them hard on the steering wheel. "All right, psycho. What do you want to know?"

"What happened after the concert you took my sister to?"

Jenny glares at me with hatred in her eyes. "You make it sound like I dragged Hannah along. She went willingly."

"I find that hard to believe. Hannah didn't like going to concerts."

"I didn't even buy the tickets. A friend we knew from school called me up and offered some tickets she wasn't using. Apparently, the guitar player is her brother, so she got them for free."

"Okay. Then what?"

"We went. It didn't cost us anything, so we figured, why not?"

"So, you watched the show, then you left. Where did you go?"

She puts her head down. Her voice lowers to a whisper. "We didn't leave afterward."

"What do you mean you didn't leave?"

Jenny takes a deep breath as if she has to prepare herself. Like what she's about to tell me is too painful to say aloud. "After the concert, the lead singer invited us into the room off the side of the stage. It was like a big dressing room, with tables and chairs and coolers filled with beer and stuff."

A sick feeling bubbles up in my gut, making me instantly nauseated. "Then what happened?"

"Then...Hannah and I sat around talking with them. They seemed larger than life to both of us. They were so wild and fun. Especially the lead singer, Rage. He took a liking to Hannah right away."

"The guy's name is Rage?"

"Not his real name, probably. But that's what he called himself."

"Keep talking."

"Well, Hannah and I hated the taste of beer, so Rage opened up a couple bottles of Coke and handed them to us. It wasn't long after that I started feeling woozy. A while later, we all left together. Hannah was hanging off Rage's arm. I could tell she was feeling woozy, too."

"That bastard drugged your drinks."

Jenny nods. "Yeah. I know that now. It was the scariest thing I'd ever been through. I felt so out of control and confused."

"What happened next?"

"We ended up in a car, somehow. I was begging them to drop us off when Rage said they had to make a quick stop first."

"What was Hannah doing?"

"Nothing. She had her head resting against the side window. I remember her saying she didn't feel well, and the driver told her not to puke in his car."

"Where did you go next?"

"To a house. A rundown place. I remember the front steps were broken."

"And? What happened next?"

She says nothing.

"Jenny?"

She shakes her head. "I don't remember."

"Bullshit."

"I swore to Hannah I'd never breathe a word."

"She's gone. The rules have changed. Tell me what happened."

She doesn't meet my eyes. "Rage took Hannah down the hall and disappeared through a door."

My chest constricts, and my breathing quickens. My poor baby sister. That pig doped her up, so she was vulnerable.

I can hear myself pant as I struggle to take a deep breath. I don't know if I can bear to listen anymore, but I must. This may be the last chance I have to find out the truth. "What else do you remember?"

A tear rolls down Jenny's cheek. "I remember slumping down on this torn sofa in the living room. The three other band guys were standing around, talking. Then, one by one, Rage called them into the room where Hannah was. I could hear her moaning and saying *no* and *stop*, but I was too weak and messed up to go to her." Jenny draws a shuddering breath. "I couldn't help her. I knew they were hurting her really bad, and I couldn't help her."

For a few long moments, I can't move. Finally, I manage to reach over and put my hand on her shaking shoulder.

Jenny sniffs up her tears. "I passed out not long after. When I came to, it was still dark outside. I got up and staggered down the hall to where I saw Rage take Hannah."

"Was she still in there?"

Jenny nods slowly. "She was lying on the bed with her jeans and top crumpled on the floor beside her. Rage was passed out next to her. I went into the room, and when I grabbed Hannah's arm, her eyes flew open, and she just started screaming. *'Please, no more! Stop!'* I told her it was okay and that I would take her home. The fear in her eyes will haunt me forever."

Overwhelming pain pierces my chest and into my heart. I put my hand over my mouth to keep from hollering. Closing my eyes for a moment, I tell myself that I need to gain control.

After a few moments, I can speak again. "Did that motherfucker Rage wake up while you were in the room?"

"Just long enough to chuckle to himself and say, *'If you stick around, we can have some more fun later.'* If I had a knife and were strong enough, I would've stabbed that fucker in the throat." She takes a deep breath. "I gathered Hannah's clothes and slowly dressed her. There were bruises already forming on the inside of her thighs. She was in really bad shape."

"And then you both left?"

"Yes. We were hanging onto each other because we were still weak from whatever Rage slipped in our drinks."

"Did you call the police?"

"No."

"Why the hell not?"

Jenny shoots me a glare with her red eyes. "Your sister wouldn't let me. I begged her. I tried everything to convince her she needed the hospital and that she should get checked out, and then we could call the police, but she was adamant. She didn't want anyone to know.

"So, we walked to a nearby park, where we sat until we felt a little stronger. Hannah was bent over and moaning in pain. I was so scared that they'd damaged her inside, but she just kept saying she'd heal on her own, that she didn't want anyone to know. That's when she made me give my word that I'd never tell a soul." Jenny rakes her hands through her hair. "I knew it was wrong to make that promise, but she seemed so broken. I just couldn't betray her. You'd have understood if you'd seen her. She needed to have that control after what they did to her."

The pain stabs my heart again. "I want to know everything you know about those fuckers."

"I don't know anything more, Lance. That was the last time I saw them." She pauses. "Until today."

"What do you mean?"

"In the bar. I was sitting with friends, and I looked over, and they were there."

"They were at the bar?" My heart thumps hard. "Is that why you got up and walked out so suddenly?"

She looks at me, confused. "How did you know I did that?"

"Because I was sitting at the bar with my friend. I saw you."

She bites her lip. "Yes. They were there." Her voice is a whisper.

"But I didn't see any other musicians in…" I trail off. I suddenly remember the guys who walked in just after Reggie when I ordered our drinks. "Were they all dressed in black, like some weird cult?"

She slowly nods.

Fuck!

Less than an hour ago, I was mere feet from the sonofabitches who raped my baby sister.

Vengeance boils up from the depths of my gut, leaving a stinging acrid taste in my mouth. I want to rip them limb from limb. I slide the keys back into the ignition. "Take me back to the bar. Right now."

She shakes her head hard. "I don't want to see them. Why do you think I left there in the first place?"

"If you don't drive, Jenny, I'll toss your ass out of here and drive myself."

She squeezes her eyes shut, then cranks the ignition. "Fine. But I think you're nuts to go back in there. Do you really think you can take all four of them at once? And even if you could, you'll get thrown out the second you start causing shit in there. Don't get me wrong, I want to see those fuckers suffer as bad as you do, but there's got to be a smarter way to—"

"Just drive." I spit the words through clenched teeth.

Everything outside the windows blurs into a multi-coloured stream as Jenny weaves in and out of traffic. The drive feels like an eternity.

Finally, Jenny pulls into Lulu's parking lot and stops the car beside the entrance. I unbuckle my belt immediately, but Jenny doesn't move. There's fear in her eyes. "As much as I'd like to see what happens next, I'm still too scared to look at their faces."

"That's fine. I understand." I reach for the handle.

"Lance."

I turn to her. She hesitates, reaches into her bag, pulls something out, and presses it into my hand. I look down and see a gold necklace. It takes a moment for me to recognize it as the necklace Hannah always wore.

"She left it in my car one day. I never got a chance to give it back."

I nod and clip it around my neck. Then I open the passenger door and climb out. Before closing the door, I lean down and meet Jenny's gaze again. "What's the name of their band?"

"They call themselves *USH*."

"USH?"

"Yeah. I think it means United Sons of Hell."

I scoff. "Idiots."

"Do you want me to wait here for a few minutes, so you'll have a ride when they throw your ass out of there?"

"Goodbye, Jenny."

I slam the door shut, and Jenny's shit-box Pinto squeals away as I make my way to the entrance. The insipid sound of canned music seeps through the crack in the door as I grab the cold handle.

I'm about to open the door when Jenny's words float through my brain. *"Do you really think you can take all four of them at once?"*

I'm not a fighter unless it's necessary to protect myself or someone else, and right now my body seethes with a vengeance so potent I can barely stand still.

I don't just want to hurt them. I want to wipe them off the face of the Earth for what they did to Hannah.

I take a deep breath and, with great effort, pull my hand off the door handle.

I need to get a hold of my emotions. Then I need to strategize. Come up with a plan of attack—an eye for an eye. But I need to be smart about it. Jenny is right—storming in with fists flailing isn't going to end the way I want it to.

It takes everything I have to turn from the door and walk away. With every step from Lulu's, I feel a cold darkness expand inside me.

About two blocks up the road, I see Jenny's Pinto coming toward me. I stop when she pulls up.

"Get in."

I hop into the passenger side and look over at her with surprise.

She shrugs. "I thought you'd be needing a ride. I'm glad you came to your senses."

Without responding, I look out the window. I begin contemplating what my next move should be.

On the way home, Jenny talks about Hannah. How, after that horrible night, she became withdrawn and depressed. "The next thing I knew, she had quit her job and was hanging out with the druggie crowd. I tried to talk to her, but the truth is, I was getting into some bad stuff myself. I wasn't in a position to be helping anyone."

"You should have reached out to me."

"I know. I thought about it. I called your mom once, but she was drunk. Halfway through our conversation, her voice dropped off. I didn't try again after that."

"Have you ever seen that band at Lulu's before? Or do you know of anyplace else they hang out?"

"I don't ever go to Lulu's, so I'm not sure if that's where they hang out. I'm telling you, I know nothing about them. Right after Hannah died, I tried to remember where their house was, but no matter how long I drove around, I could never find it."

I let out a disappointed sigh. "Well, let me know if you see them again or remember anything else."

We pull up in front of the house. I grab the door handle, but Jenny puts a hand on my arm before I get out. "Lance, what are you planning on doing? Are you going to fuck them up?" When I don't answer, she continues in a low voice, "I hope so. I want to help. I want to see every one of them suffer."

"Just call if you remember anything more." I get out of the car and, without turning back, walk to the house.

* * *

Country music blares from the living room. Not the good kind, with an uplifting beat and catchy rhythm, but the slow, crying-in-your-beer type a person would play shortly before jumping off a bridge.

I kick off my runners and walk into the front room to see Mom sitting in the La-Z-Boy, a full glass of clear liquid in her hand. Her head wobbles as she turns and looks up at me. I watch her lips as she mouths something, but the music is so loud her voice gets swallowed up. I walk over, grab the remote, and press the mute button.

"Where the hell were you?" she slurs.

I tell her I went for a walk to the park, omitting everything else that had happened since I left the house. "Maybe you should try to eat something, Mom. The neighbour, Kim, came by and brought over a casserole."

"That woman can't cook. The only thing she does well is gossip. You can toss out whatever crap she made."

"Come on, Mom. She obviously went to some effort into preparing us a meal. The least we can do is try it."

"I'm not interested. Besides, I'm not the least bit hungry."

"Well, I won't let a home-cooked meal go to waste."

I turn and walk into the kitchen, and just as I open the cupboard door, the gloomy country music resumes. I shake my head as I grab a plate, then go to the fridge and spoon out some of the now-congealed casserole. After I heat the food in the microwave for a few minutes, I take my plate and head for the stairs, giving my mother a nod as I pass through the living room.

Sitting on my bed in my room, I spoon the thick, rubbery cheese from the top of the casserole and gather a small mound of pasta into my mouth. It only takes a few swirls inside my mouth before my mother's words are confirmed. *This does taste like crap.*

Still, I've eaten a lot worse while on the road gigging, and since there's no other food in front of me, I continue to ingest the barely edible concoction. As I chew hard, I look around the room at the old soccer trophies and ribbons I won in high school. On the opposing wall are posters of bands I was obsessed with in my late teens—Winger, Cinderella, and Whitesnake. Bands that none of my friends were into. None except for Reggie. He listened to the same '80s and '90s music as me. Everyone else was into pop-rock or rap—genres I could never wrap my head around. That link, that commonality of music, made us friends. I remember driving around in Dad's car on the weekends. I would roll up to an intersection where there was always a car full of people with the windows down and the shittiest tunes blaring from their stereo.

When I finish the last morsel of the plastic-textured macaroni, I lean over to put the plate on my dresser and notice the small pink pompom bunny that Hannah had so proudly made for me when she was in elementary school. I pick it up and slowly roll it in my fingers. One of its googly glued-on eyes is half-coming off, and the once-poofy white tail is now flat.

I remember the day she gave this to me. There was the sound of the school bus pulling away from the curb outside, and Mom and I were cleaning out the fireplace when Hannah burst through the door with her hand extended, the little bunny resting carefully in her palm. "I made this special for you, Lance."

With black soot covering my hands, I had to quickly wash before she would let me have my gift.

"It's a special bunny. If you're ever having a bad day, you just have to hold him in your hand, and you'll feel better." Her eyes were as big as saucers as she gazed convincingly into my eyes. She was so full of magic and excitement back then. So fun to be around. It was hard to be in a bad mood around Hannah, even during her pre-teen hormonal phase. I'd heard about it being a miserable time of anger and insolence, but the only change I noticed with Hannah was that she would cry easier—at almost everything. Other than that, she was the same well-mannered girl.

Suddenly pain shoots through my temple and pressure accumulates behind my eyes—damn headaches. When I turned twenty-five, I quit getting what the doctor diagnosed as *cluster headaches*. It's the first time since then that there's been a threat of having another.

I go to the bathroom and open the cupboard above the sink. As I scan the rows of prescription bottles in my search for Aspirin, I focus on some labels. Ativan. Percocet. Demerol. What in the hell are these doing in here? I look closer. Every tag on every bottle has my mother's name on it.

I shake my head. I can't believe the arsenal of drugs she has in here and wonder if her doctors are aware that she's washing all this shit down with multiple bottles of booze. Her situation is even more fucked-up than I had initially thought.

Perfect! Just perfect. This discovery puts the cherry on the cake.

Foregoing my search for Aspirin, I return to my room, rifle through the top drawer of my old desk until I find a pad of paper and a pen, then sit on my bed.

My hand sketches before my mind wills it to. Soon, the word *revenge* appears in big, lightning-shaped letters at the top of the page.

Because of one night, I lost not only the best person in my life, but grief and trauma have also taken my mother. I have no one left. No one whole, anyway. And for that, I will make those soulless bastards pay.

Every last one of them.

I write the letters *USH* over and over on the paper. I've got to find out more about these dirtbags, but how?

Jenny told me everything she could remember, and it wasn't much, definitely not enough to hatch a plan. What I need is to somehow get in close to them. Only then will I be able to find their weak points. I'm sure the rest will come to me after that.

My mother coughs from downstairs. If she had any idea what I was planning, I know a part of her would be overjoyed, but the rest would think I was being ridiculous, that I should call the cops and let them handle it.

I'd never do that. Not because I don't like cops. I respect the hell out of them, considering all the low lives they deal with every day. My issues are with the judicial system. I can see it now: I'd tell the cops what I know and maybe even talk—or threaten— Jenny into testifying. Then the prosecution would spend a month compiling their case, only to have it thrown out due to lack of physical evidence. Or, at most, each of the rapists would get a slap on the wrist before being released due to a lack of space in the penitentiaries.

I can't risk that. If I take matters into my own hands, I am the police, the judge, and the executioner. They won't have a chance to plead their cases. They won't be able to make excuses about their sad upbringings and how the lack of breaks they had growing up led them to rape my little sister.

Nope, fuck that. My ears will be closed, along with my mind. Nothing will get in the way of what I must do—an eye for an eye.

Chapter 3

After getting my mother to eat a half bowl of chicken noodle soup from a can, I help her to bed. Then, when I'm alone in the living room, I sit in Dad's chair and resume plotting my next move.

A few hours pass with me staring at the page. The only move I can come up with is returning to where I last saw the band. Lulu's.

Tomorrow, I will get up early and call a couple of alcohol counseling numbers. Not that I believe for one minute Mom will admit she has a problem or agree to get help for it, but it's a start. After that, I'll stop by Lulu's bar before the lunch rush, as I did today. With any luck, the black-clad band pukes will make an appearance.

I spend the rest of the night doing Google and YouTube searches for the band USH, but not surprisingly, nothing comes up.

* * *

Zurich is the place to be on so many levels—the outgoing people, the architectural beauty, and, of course, the shopping. But Europe can't compete with all of West Vancouver's treasures.

I wake to the smell of the giant Douglas fir trees outside my window. Sparrows and crows sit high on the majestic branches, singing and squawking as they peer down at the earth below. The strong scent of the Pacific Ocean wafts into my window on the morning breeze. It's no wonder Vancouver hosts millions of tourists every year. As much as I loved it overseas, I've really missed the beauty of home.

I slowly climb out of bed, stretch, and head for the bedroom door when I hear glass shattering downstairs. Worried that my mother has hurt herself, I fling open the door and sprint down the steps.

When I reach the bottom and look through the entranceway to the kitchen, Mom is standing in front of the cupboard with a stack of plates in her hand. On the floor, pieces of broken glass surround her bare feet.

"What in the hell is going on?"

She looks up at me and, at first glance, seems sober. "I've always hated these damn plates. Your father's mother gave us these as a wedding gift. I never liked the woman or her taste in dishes."

"So why break them? Just put them in a box and donate them or something."

"Why? So someone else can get saddled with the ugly things?"

No sooner do the words leave her mouth than she raises the stack above her head and throws the dishes at the ground with whatever power her frail body can muster. The impact makes a hell of a racket as they burst into hundreds of sharp fragments around her.

"Mom, don't move. I'm going to come over and get you."

"Don't worry, Lance. If I cut myself, I won't feel it. I can't feel anything since my sweet little girl died." Tears run down her gaunt, ashen face.

I put my hand up. "I know, Mom. I know you feel really bad. I get it. But I'm asking you to stay still until I get you out of the glass. After that, we'll sit down together and talk, okay?"

"I don't deserve to be rescued. I couldn't even save my own child. I'm nothing more than garbage." With her eyes still focused on mine, I hear a crunching sound as she steps forward onto the sea of broken glass.

"Mom! Stop!"

Now, knowing that she's taken leave of her senses, my plan to sweep the glass first so I can remove her safely goes out the back door—I'm thrust into an act-quick situation.

The first step I take onto the glass earns me my initial cut; a long shard enters my heel. More worried for my mother than myself, I grit my teeth and move forward. Her posture tells me she's ready to move again. I put my arms out in front of me, not quite able yet to touch her. "Stay where you are."

She slowly grins, then shakes her head. "Watch your feet, son. You could get cut."

I take another step. This stride is longer, so the gap between us shortens faster. "Are you hungry? I can make you something good after this. Whatever you want." My words are intentional. I know the last thing on her mind is food, but my goal is to distract her.

"I'm not hungry. I don't care if I ever eat again."

She looks down at the floor, then raises her foot. I lunge toward her. When I step down, a big piece of glass pushes between my toes and cuts into me like a hot knife through butter.

Willing myself to move past the pain, I grab my mother's toothpick-thin arm, preventing her from moving. I then wrap my free arm around her waist and lift her feet a few inches off the floor. With my mom secured, I make the painful walk back through shattered glass.

Finally, we reach the soft carpet, and I set her down. "What were you thinking?"

She drops her eyes to the floor. "Look at the blood you got on the carpet, Lance. I don't think I'll ever be able to get that out."

I let out a deep sigh. "I don't give a shit about the carpet. I care about you, and you're acting like a complete wacko."

Mom immediately meets my eyes with a stern glare. She's about to lecture me, I can tell but then pauses. Instead of reprimanding me for what I said, she puts her hands over her face and lets out a sob. "I can't do this anymore, Lance. I want to be with Hannah."

I gently hug her and then lift her up in my arms. "It's going to be okay. I promise."

I carry her to the bathroom and flip the toilet lid down before setting her on it. When I crouch down to look for the first-aid kit under the sink, I see my bloody footprints on the white tile floor.

Once I locate the small red kit, I run water over a wad of toilet paper and kneel in front of my mother to tend to her cuts. I gently lift one foot and wipe away the blood to see the degree of her wounds.

"I drink too much," she blurts out.

For a moment, I stop what I'm doing. "Yeah, I know. How long have you been going hard?"

"Quite a while now, ever since Hannah started to change. I bought my first bottle of vodka when she didn't come home one evening. I made us a nice dinner and rented a movie. I think it was called *Postcards from the Edge*. You know, the one with Meryl Streep and that other actress?"

I shake my head, grinning. "Sounds like a chick flick to me, Mom." I continue gently cleaning her foot.

"Well, it was one Hannah chose, and I'd never seen it, so I rented it online."

"And she stood you up?"

Mom nods. "She was doing that a lot then. Sometimes I wouldn't see or hear from her for days—it was horrible. You have no idea how stressful that is for a parent. I didn't know where she was or if she was okay. For all I knew, she was holed up somewhere with dangerous people around her."

If you only knew how close you were to the truth, Mom.

"Anyway, it was during that time I bought my first bottle. I remember bringing the vodka home and sitting at the kitchen table with the bottle in front of me. I poured about an inch into a glass and slowly took a sip. It was like fire on my lips and made me cough. I hated it but hated the way I felt more. I was in such a distraught state and all alone."

"You didn't have to be alone."

"We've already discussed that, Lance. I told you why I felt I couldn't call you. I couldn't take you coming home and freaking out about Hannah despite what I was already going through with her."

There's a small piece of glass sticking out of her heel. I lean over and open the vanity drawer to grab the tweezers.

"The vodka tasted awful, but I knew I would go numb if I could get enough down. That's the exact feeling I needed—numbness."

I position her heel in the light, then carefully use the tweezers to latch onto the sliver of glass and pull it out.

Without flinching, she continues, "Then I remembered something my mother would say when making us swallow cod liver oil. *Plug your nose when you swallow, and you won't taste it.* I tried that, and while it helped with the taste, it didn't help the burning. I still kept trying, though. It got easier. Eventually, the vodka slipped down as easy as water."

"And was it worth it? Did you feel better?"

"In the beginning, I sure did. But then I started forgetting important things. Appointments. Dates. I was concerned about it at first but eventually stopped caring. After a while, the only task I could manage was making sure I didn't run out of booze."

"And what about the pills? I found a hell of a lot in the cabinet."

She moves her eyes to the wall, where a small framed picture of flowers hangs. I can tell she's feeling ashamed.

I reach into the first aid bag and grab a couple bandages, which I use to cover her superficial cuts. Then I wet another wad of tissue to wipe down her other foot. "Mom. Talk to me. It's okay. I'm not judging you here."

She shakes her head. "I've become such a failure. I've let everyone down, especially Hannah."

"That's not true. You never let Hannah down. The only life you can control is your own."

She turns her face toward mine. "Don't lie to me, son. I raised you to be honest and speak your truth. And don't lessen how far down I've let myself go. I am a bag of garbage, and you know it!"

"Well, you may feel you're at the point of no return, but I don't see it that way. At least you admitted that you have a problem. That's a healthy sign. Besides, you're not as far down as you think. There are a lot of people who are going through the same thing."

She scoffs. "Really? There are a lot of people who just lost their child—their innocent, beautiful child—to drugs and are now addicted themselves?"

"I'm not saying each person's story is exactly the same, but you can bet a lot of alcoholics drink to forget traumatic things they went through. It's called self-medicating. Right now, the only thing you should think about is whether you've had enough of the booze and pills. Ask yourself—do you want to get better? Or are you going to continue destroying yourself?"

She lets out a laugh. "You sound so wise, Lance. How did I ever give birth to such a wise child?" She reaches out and gently strokes my cheek. "I love you, son. I'm sorry you lost your baby sister, and I'm sorry you had to come home to me in this condition."

"I understand, Mom. But all we have left now is each other. We must both try our best to be healthy, okay?"

She nods. "I know. You're right. We're no longer the Three Musketeers. We're down to two now. And as depressed as I sometimes feel—a lot of the time—it would be pretty selfish to drink myself into an early grave and leave you all alone."

Thankfully, her second foot has barely any cuts. It only takes a few bandages to cover them. I stand up, gather the wrappers and tissue, and throw them into the trash.

"Thank you, Lance. Thank you for fixing me up. Now, it's your turn. I'll trade you places so I can look at the damage to your feet."

"I'll be fine, Mom. I don't think I'm cut very badly."

She looks at my bloody footprints on the floor. "I think you're wrong, son. There's blood everywhere."

"I'll tell you what. I'll help you downstairs to your chair, and then I'll clean off my feet. After that, maybe we can talk about what to do next."

"I don't need your help, dear. I'll manage fine myself. Plus, I need to sweep up that awful mess in the kitchen."

It takes a few minutes to convince her not to go into the kitchen and to let me be the one to clean up the broken glass. She gets up and slowly limps toward the bathroom door.

"I'm sorry you got cut because of me. I promise not to go crazy like that again."

"Don't worry about it, Mom. Besides, something good did come out of your rage."

She stops in the doorway and looks back at me. "What's that?"

"You finally got rid of the dishes you hated so much."

As soon as she's gone, I turn the bathtub faucet on and stick my feet into the water, which instantly turns pink. I'm cut much worse than Mom and feel skin flapping between my toes.

Sure enough, as soon as I sit on the tub edge and inspect the bottoms of my feet, I'm shocked at the depth of some cuts. My soles look like I got attacked with a straight razor. Normally, I would go to the emergency department to get stitches, but I don't want to leave Mom while she's so vulnerable. I've got to stay and try to get her some help.

I grit my teeth from the stinging pain as the water runs over my feet. Then I grab a hand towel and carefully dry them off. Thankfully, I find a few butterfly bandages in the first-aid kit and can tape together most of my cuts enough to stop the bleeding.

I mop up the blood from the floor, rinse out the tub, then head downstairs to help my mother devise a recovery plan. I'm so blown away that she actually admitted to having a problem. Now, we must find a solution before she changes her mind.

* * *

Since neither of us has ever been in this situation before, I go online and research support groups for alcoholics. I've heard of people getting the DTs when they quit drinking. I'm just not sure what exactly that means, or if it can be dangerous.

I find lists of AA resources online, but every link opens to details about the 12-Step Program. I'm sure this information will be useful at one point but not now.

I glance at Mom. She appears tired and anxious. I need to come up with options for her quickly. I turn my attention back to the screen and scroll faster.

"Lance, maybe you should forget about the internet and take me to the hospital."

I turn back to her, shocked. "That's a great idea. I didn't think you'd be open to going there."

"I have nothing to lose at this point. It's not like they'll do anything to make me feel worse than I already do."

I can't believe how easy she's accepting the situation. Thank God she's reached her current mindset; having no booze in her system right now must give her some clarity—another reason to act fast.

With Mom loaded in the passenger seat of Dad's car, I slide into the driver's seat and slowly back out of the driveway. Kim is trimming her hedges and looks over at the car, waving. I wave back, and in my peripheral vision, I see my mother flipping the bird at the window.

"Mom. Did you just give Kim the finger?"

She grins devilishly. "No. I was trying to wave, but only one finger would cooperate."

"You're a very bad girl." I shake my head and chuckle.

* * *

The Hospital Emergency entrance is situated on a narrow two-lane road with the fire department and police station directly across from it. Any time I've been here, it takes forever to find parking. Then, when I finally do locate a spot, I go inside and discover the packed emergency room. No matter the time of day, it's always standing room only.

I swing the car through the patient drop-off area, where two ambulances are stopped directly in front of us. "Mom, you should get out here. I'll find somewhere to park and meet you inside."

I can tell she's nervous by the scowl on her face. She slowly climbs out of the car and heads toward the entrance.

It takes about ten minutes for the ambulances to leave. I then start the long, aggravating task of circling the lot for somewhere to park. Finally, after about twenty minutes, an elderly lady in a Prius pulls out of a spot about a half block from the hospital.

When I finally step through the automatic doors of the emergency department, I look across the busy room and spot Mom sitting at a small stall, talking to a woman tapping on a keyboard behind a computer. I walk up behind my mother and put a hand on her shoulder. When she turns to look at me, I can tell she's been crying. It's a hard situation for her, I'm sure.

She asks me to sit in the waiting room until she's finished talking with the lady. That's a good sign. She hasn't given up on getting help yet.

I sit on one of the curved white seats affixed to the floor. Across from me is an elderly couple. The woman is in a wheelchair with a hospital band on her wrist, and her husband's hand rests on her knee. Sitting beside the pair is a woman, about fifty. She has no teeth, and her gaunt face is cratered in, making her eyes look like they're popping out of her head. Her legs are shaking, and she's fidgety. A drug addict, if I had to guess.

She notices me looking at her and smiles. I smile back. I realize Hannah never had longevity in her addiction. She was still a part of the same world as this woman.

I wonder about this woman and if her mother worries about her. I wonder how badly it's affected her loved ones, as Hannah's addiction has affected Mom and me.

A few minutes later, I see Mom wearing a hospital wristband and heading toward me.

"What did they tell you, Mom?"

She sits next to me. "Nothing. They just took my information and put me in the queue to see a doctor. She said we probably won't have to wait long."

"It doesn't matter how long it takes. This is the best place for us to be right now." I grab a magazine from a nearby table and hand it to Mom. I figure it's probably best she occupies her brain so she's not spending time questioning her decision to come here.

While Mom flips through the pages of the tabloid mag, the emergency door opens, and a stretcher wheels in by two ambulance attendants.

As they roll past, I look at the patient, a girl with multi-coloured hair and lots of costume jewelry—a barbed wire bracelet and thick silver neck chains. She wears a facemask hooked up to an oxygen bottle.

The attendants stop walking when a nurse with a clipboard greets them. Because of the noise in the room, I can't quite hear what's being said. I'm about to turn away when the nurse asks for the girl's first name. I'm able to make out what the attendant says, *Jennifer*.

My eyes fly back to the patient's bright, multi-coloured hair. I stand up. "Mom. I think that girl on the stretcher is Hannah's friend. I think that's Jenny."

Mom diverts her attention from the magazine to the stretcher. "Why do you say that? You haven't seen her in years. You don't even know what she looks like now."

"She was at Hannah's funeral. Don't you remember? I only spoke to her for a moment, but I remember that hair. And one of the ambulance people just said, *Jennifer*."

Doubt clears from my mother's face, leaving her looking disturbed. "Should you go and speak to them?"

"No. Whatever is happening with the girl, they don't need me sticking my nose into things."

"I have her parents' number in my cellphone contacts. I could give them a shout. They called to give their condolences when they found out about Hannah." My mother reaches into her purse and pulls out an ancient cell phone.

"I don't think you should, Mom. What if you get caught up in conversation when the nurse calls your name?"

My mother pauses her finger over the keypad. "If Hannah was taken to the hospital, and someone I knew had seen her, I'd want them to call me."

I sigh and hold out my hand. "I'll tell you what—give me your phone, and I'll call them. This girl might not even be their Jenny, so I'll be careful how I word things. I don't want to frighten them if she's not their daughter."

Mom presses the phone into my hand. I scroll through her contacts until I find the contact: *Jenny (Parents)*. I hit *call* , put the phone to my ear, and then head down a quiet corridor.

An older-sounding woman answers. I explain who I am, and she immediately tells me how sorry she is about Hannah's death. I thank her, then ask if she has spoken to her daughter recently.

"I spoke to Jenny last night. She was at a party. At least, that's what it sounded like in the background. She said she'd call me today, but I haven't heard from her yet. Why do you ask?"

I tell her that I'm at the hospital emergency department. "Someone was just wheeled in on a stretcher, and she looks a lot like your daughter."

At first, there's a long pause. Then, "I'm not surprised she's there." The woman's voice is shaking. "If it is her, she's probably overdosed again. And if that's the case, it'll be the third time she's done this over the past six months." She draws a deep, shuddering breath. "We've gotten to a point where we're not surprised by anything she does anymore."

"I'm so sorry. You and your husband have been through a lot. I'm sure it hasn't been easy."

"It's no different than what your poor mother had to endure with your sister. Although, I don't think Hannah had to be taken to the hospital as often as Jennifer."

"To be honest with you, I'm not sure. I've been away for quite a while and wasn't told anything about my sister."

Again, there is a long pause. Then, "Why are you at the emergency room? Is everything all right?"

I tell her my mother is suffering from flu-like symptoms. "I'm sure it's nothing to worry about. We're just being careful." I'm sure Jenny's mother has all the best intentions, but if the truth about Mom somehow leaked, it would spread like crazy amongst the West Vancouver hens.

Jenny's mother sighs into the phone. "I'll give Jenny a call, then the hospital if she doesn't answer. If she's there, my husband and I will come down, again."

I end the call, then head back to where Mom is sitting and tell her about the conversation.

"Did she ask why we're here?" Her tone is laced with concern.

I nod. "Don't worry, Mom. I didn't spill the beans. I just said you had the flu."

"Are they coming down here?"

"If they confirm it's their daughter."

"I hope I'm long gone by then. The last thing I need is someone recognizing me here."

I turn and watch a male nurse wheel the girl on the cot through a set of heavy doors. In my gut, I know it's Jenny. As much as I loathe that she never found a way to help Hannah, I feel sick. But she's young, and there's still hope for her given the right opportunities for rehabilitation.

I hand Mom her phone, and she slides it into her purse as a nurse comes into the waiting area and calls my mother's name. I help Mom stand and walk with her toward the nurse.

The nurse consults her clipboard, then directs her attention at me. "The doctor will need to examine your mother first. After that, we'll call you in."

Mom turns and looks up at me. "Don't worry, Lance. I'll be fine." Her fearful and uncertain eyes clash hard with her words.

With a sigh, I sit back down as the nurse leads my mother down a short, white hallway. I note my mother's fragility as her tiny, spindly legs carry her waifish body down the hall. She looks like she would fall over at the slightest wind. After battering the shit out of herself, consuming all those pills and booze, it's hard to believe she's lasted this long. But she's in the best place she can be right now. I can only hope something good comes out of it.

* * *

It's a good hour before the nurse returns to tell me I can join my mother now.

As we head down the white hallway, all noise from the waiting room muffles behind us. Soon, all I hear is the squeak of the nurse's shoes as she walks in front of me. As

I follow, I get a couple of shooting pains in my heels. It's the first time since our arrival at the hospital that I feel the pain of my cut-up feet.

On the third floor, the nurse opens a door and a waft of industrial cleaner hits me. Mom is sitting on a metal-framed chair at the foot of the bed with her head down.

"The doctor will be back shortly." The nurse closes the door.

As soon as we're alone, Mom looks up at me. Her eyes are tired and full of worry.

"What's wrong, Mom? Did something happen?"

She slowly shakes her head. "I'm starting to feel a lot worse. I can't stop my hands from shaking."

I walk up beside her and pat her shoulder. "You've taken the hardest step by coming here. I'm sure the doctor will help with what you're feeling."

Hoping I'm right, I shift her attention from worrying about her current state. "I noticed the lawn is looking a bit shabby. Do you usually get someone to do the yard work?"

She shrugs. "I used to pay the boy to mow the grass, but lately, I've just been letting it go. I can't imagine what the neighbours must think. Their lawns are always so perfectly manicured." She rubs her face with a shaking hand. "I used to spend so much time and money keeping everything outside beautiful and aesthetic. I couldn't even get it together this year to plant flowers."

"That's okay, Mom. I'll fix it for you. I need to work on my tan, anyway."

She forces a smile as the door opens, and the doctor, a man about my age, enters. He regards my mother kindly. "How are we doing now?"

"I'm starting to feel pretty rough."

"That's expected. I can help with the symptoms you're feeling. However, I think it's a good idea to stay in hospital for a night or two, so we can monitor and help you stabilize."

Mom's eyes widen, and she shifts her focus from the doctor to me. "I don't want to stay in this place, Lance. Can't I just go home? You'll be there. You can watch me—"

"I know you're nervous," the doctor interrupts, "but I promise, we'll take great care of you here. I don't recommend you leave the hospital. You are at risk of having seizures. If you're in the hospital, we'll make sure your body is strong enough to fight the withdrawals."

"He's right, Mom. You're far better off here, getting the care you need. It's just until you're feeling stronger. If something happened to you at home, it would take a long time for the ambulance to come, and I'd never forgive myself." I lay a hand on her bony shoulder. "I'll come in every day to visit. I promise. And if you're really good, I'll ask Kim for some of her yummy casserole." I give Mom a playful wink.

The doctor turns his attention to me for the first time since walking into the room. "We will start an IV for hydration. Then we'll give her anti-seizure medication and something to help her sleep."

I nod, then look at Mom. "Is that okay?"

She doesn't answer.

"It's just for a short time, Mom. Do you think you can handle it?"

"If I have to, I guess," she mutters.

The doctor reassures her she's doing the right thing, then says he'll send in a nurse to start the IV. After giving Mom a quick pat on the hand, he turns to me and asks to speak outside.

I follow the doctor into the hallway, where he gives orders to a nurse regarding Mom, then turns back to me. His expression is far more serious than when he was addressing my mother.

"It's good that you brought her when you did. Her blood pressure is high, and she's very dehydrated. I've ordered bloodwork to get a better understanding of what else is going on."

I take a deep breath. "But she'll be okay, right?"

"At this point, I can't say. Some of the tests I'm ordering will show the state of her kidneys. After that, we'll know more about what we're dealing with."

I cross my arms. "Let's just say that everything checks out with her bloodwork. What happens then?"

"If there's no permanent damage, we will stabilize her and get some nutrients into her. Once she's stable, we'll send the social worker to discuss options."

"What do you mean, options?"

"She'll need to arrange for going to detox and meet with a counselor. After she returns home, provided she's well enough, she'll receive a call once there's room for her at detox."

I nod. "In the meantime, while she's here, you'll keep her out of pain and relaxed?"

"I'll do my best."

I thank him, then go back into the room. My mother is sitting in the same position, staring out the window. I walk up and touch her arm. "Are you okay?"

"I've certainly been better."

The door opens again, and a cheerful-looking nurse enters, pushing an IV pole. "Hi, folks. We'll need all the boys in the room to leave now—we've got to put a gown on and get the IV hooked up."

I look back at Mom, unsure. "You want me to return when the nurse finishes?"

"No, I think you should go home, son. I'll be okay. I have my cell phone in my purse if I need you."

* * *

In the hallway, I feel like shit for leaving her. The only peace of mind I have comes from the doctor's promise to make her feel better. At least with the hospital's medication, she won't feel so shaky and freaked out. Still, I'm deserting her.

As I walk through the emergency department, I scan the faces I pass to find Jenny's parents but have no luck. Even if they were here, I probably wouldn't recognize them. It's been too many years.

Chapter 4

A cold feeling washes over me when I enter the house. It used to be a place always filled with Hannah's and my mother's joyful presence. Now, there is only silence.

I head for the living room. Just as I reach the La-Z-Boy, I glance into the kitchen and see the sea of glass still on the floor. *Shit*.

For a moment, I'm tempted to leave the mess, at least for a while. However, with so much stuff whizzing through my mind, I know I'll thoughtlessly walk in there to grab a drink and cut the shit out of my feet again. I'd better deal with it now.

Mentally exhausted from everything that's happened today, I trudge over to the hall closet, grab the broom and dustpan, then head for the kitchen to finish the work Mom didn't.

* * *

By the time I've meticulously swept and mopped up every visible sliver of glass, I feel the same way about the dishes as Mom did— I hate every last broken piece. Thankfully, I got only a few slivers in my fingers during the clean-up process. Slivers that, although I can't see, I'm sure I'll feel the next time I play guitar.

I take a quick peek into the fridge for something to stave off growing hunger pains, but the only thing I see is the rubber casserole Kim made—a hard pass.

Flopping down in the La-Z-Boy, my body melts into the old, worn chair. I remember when Dad bought this recliner. I was just a kid. He'd come home from work, I'd crawl up on his lap, and we would sit here together, watching Columbo while Mom made dinner.

I pull my cell phone from my pocket and double-check that I haven't missed a call from Mom. But the only new notification is a text from Erik, the engineer from the studio in Zurich where I did sessions, asking if I was planning to return.

I miss being there and working with a great group of guys. After long days, the musicians and everyone else in the studio would wander over to The Broken Fiddle pub for a good meal and many hours of talking shop. I felt in my element there. Granted, the apartment I rented was small with noisy pipes, but the neighbours were great and minded their own business. Unlike here, where everyone knows what you've done before you've got your pants up. The people of Zurich are far more open-minded and accepting. My kind of place. I'm itching to go back, but I've got a lot of business to take care of here before I can even consider jumping on another plane.

I'm hungry and should order something, but somewhere between searching online for a restaurant that delivers and scrolling through menus, I doze off...

* * *

The dark brick walls close in as my eyes fixate on the distant figure walking ahead in the alleyway.

"Don't do it, Lance." Hannah's voice floats from beside me, pleading. "Let him go."

"Shh. Keep your voice down, or he'll hear us."

We pass under a buzzing neon sign. Hannah grasps my arm with her hand, spindly and cold. I glance at her, then jerk my arm away when I see that half of her face is missing, with only rotting flesh hanging from the bones of her jaw.

I'm frozen in place, unable to take my eyes off her. "Hannah, your face..."

She tilts her head, or what's left of it. "Why are you looking at me like that?"

Horrified, I can do nothing but stare.

There's a clatter at the far end of the alley, followed by an eerie laugh that echoes down the narrow lane. *He's getting away.*

I turn back to Hannah, but she's gone.

My eyes fly open. My heart thumps in my ears. Gasping, I put my hand on my chest. Something is buzzing—my phone. I look around the room in a panic, then slowly remember where I am.

I force in a deep breath, then exhale slowly to calm my nerves. That was the most terrifying nightmare I can remember having. All I see is Hannah's grotesque face. She looked like a character in a zombie movie. And who was I following in the alleyway?

Whoever it was, I remember feeling obsessed with catching him. I can only assume he was connected to the pigs that raped my little sister.

I catch the call on the fourth ring, just before it goes to voicemail. "Hello." I'm out of breath.

"Hey, man, it's Reg. Did I catch you at a bad time? You sound like you were jogging or something."

I sit forward in the chair and rub my eyes with my free hand. "It's all good. I was doing some work around the house. What's up?"

"I just heard that Lulu's has a band tonight. They're called Snake Oil. I know the lead singer, Darren. He used to play for Harlequin before moving to the States and starting his own band. Anyways, I thought I could convince you to come out, seeing as you ditched me the other day." He laughs.

Leaving the house risks not being home when Mom calls, but something tells me she'll be busy feeling like shit for a while. Besides, after the nightmare I just had, I could use a distraction. "Yeah, okay. I'm in."

Reg says he'll pick me up in an hour, so I use the time to shower and change the bandages on my feet. With five minutes to spare, I quickly try Mom's cell number. I'm not surprised when she doesn't answer. Hopefully, they have her sedated, and she's getting some rest.

I leave her a brief supportive voicemail, then head out of the house to wait for Reg.

* * *

As we approach the club, we hear DJ music with thumping subfrequencies from inside. If it's this loud out here, it must be really pumping inside.

A line-up of about ten people waits at the door. It's a huge surprise to Reg, who says he hasn't seen this kind of attendance in years. "It's because of Snake Oil's following online. I swear, man, nobody pays much attention if you aren't tied into social media."

Reg knows the temporary bouncer from a club downtown; he lets us in ahead of everyone else. As predicted, there's a DJ freestyling with vinyl in the corner. His hat is on backward, and he has a tattoo of a snake covering half his face and wrapping around his neck.

The place is booming—a one-eighty-degree difference from the other day when Reg and I had lunch here. We walk past the stage, where a drum tech and a few other guys tweak the lights.

Reg points to the back of the room, where a small round table sits near the entrance to the john. When we sit down, our chairs touch. Reg raises an eyebrow. "Wow, is this the kiddie table?"

"We look like we're on a date."

Reg snorts. "Just so you know ahead of time, I ain't putting out, no matter how many rounds you buy."

"Frigid, are we?"

We laugh just as the waitress walks up and takes our order. She's cute, so we both lean as far from each other as possible.

Scoping out the room as we wait for our beer, it doesn't take long to realize we're among the oldest dudes in the room. Everyone else looks like they've just gotten out of high school.

"It's like we're chaperones," I say.

"Yeah, what a colossal mistake that would be, huh?"

When the band takes the stage, the room erupts in applause. The lead singer, Darren Moore, grabs the mic and greets the room, then turns and cues the band. As soon as the first guitar chords ring out, the crowd recognizes the tune and goes wild— "Vampire." Arguably one of their best. I remember seeing the video for this song recently. It kicked ass.

The last I heard, Snake Oil was planning a European tour. As a hard rock band, they'll do a hell of a lot better on the other side of the pond than they will here in North America. The music industry has been drying up in Canada and the States for years. Everything is online here, whereas overseas, original bands still have a chance to peak.

We drink one beer after another as we watch the show and try to hear the music through the screams of fans.

As Snake Oil wraps up the show, droves of drunk fans filter out of the bar. Reg stands up. "Be back. Gonna take a whiz."

While I wait for him to return, I look over what's left of Lulu's patrons. Other than the tables near the stage, almost everyone has filed out of the bar. The DJ is in his booth, packing up, when a thin guy with stringy black hair approaches him. The two start talking, and I fixate on the dark-haired guy.

Reg walks out of the john just as the guy turns our way. As soon as I see his face, I place him. It's one of the guys from USH, United Sons of Hell, or whatever bizarre name they call themselves.

"Hey, man, ready to roll? I'll drop you off at home. I've got an early day tomorrow."

I keep my eyes glued to the man talking to the DJ. "Thanks, man. But I think I'm gonna have another beer or two. You go ahead. I can find my way home."

Reg pats me on the shoulder and tells me to keep in touch. As soon as he leaves the bar, I stand up and slowly make my way over to the DJ booth.

As I approach, the DJ resumes packing up and the stringy-haired guy makes to walk away. "Hey." I jog up with a smile. "Don't I know you from somewhere?"

He looks me up and down. "Rage."

Immediately, my blood boils. "Oh yeah. Rage. And you're with that cool band, USH, right?"

"Yeah. That's right."

"Cool. Cool. I saw you guys play a while back. You were rad."

"Oh, really? Where did you see us?"

I struggle to think of an answer. "I think it was downtown at the...um..." He stares at me. A sweat breaks out on my forehead.

"Oh," he blurts out. "You mean Chases Bar on Richards?"

Relief washes over me. "Yeah, yeah. That's the place. You guys killed it."

"Thanks, man." He sticks out a hand. "Always nice to meet a fan."

It takes everything in me to reach out a hand and grasp his. "I'm Lance."

"Do you want to come to the table and meet the rest of the band?"

I force a grin. "That would be great."

As I let Rage lead the way, a sickening feeling overtakes me. I just shook the hand of the scum-sucking pig that raped my little sister. As we pass the dirty tables, my eyes lock onto the empty beer bottles left. I imagine grabbing one, busting it open on the table, and driving it deep into Rage's back.

But I can't. I have to bide my time and get close to them. Then, I can strategically make them pay—one by one.

We reach the corner table by the stage, where the remaining three USH musicians are seated.

"Hey, guys." Rage sits down. "This is Lance." He motions for me to take a seat next to him.

I can tell by the scowls on the band members' faces that they think they're superior. A guy with a black mohawk and thick black eyeliner scoffs. "Are you a musician?"

"Yeah, I play guitar sometimes."

I'm so glad Reg can't see me right now. Although we have vast musical interests in many genres, glam-goth was never high on the list. He'd probably laugh his ass off if he saw me sitting with a table of black latex-wearing posers with attitudes. If it weren't for Hannah, I wouldn't get within ten miles of these smug little pricks. It's not that I'm against their type of music—I hate it when talent comes secondary, and attitude comes first.

Another bandmate looks at Rage. "Why is he here?"

"He's a fan of ours."

"Yeah. You guys are great!" I nod vigorously.

With that, the three seem to relax. Soon, they resume talking to each other.

I turn to Rage. "So, what did you think of Snake Oil?"

"They were okay, but we're better."

"Well, that goes without saying." Inside, I'm laughing at the ridiculousness of his statement.

The mohawk guy looks across the table at me. "Do you know our names?"

I shake my head.

He points to his scrawny chest. "I'm Blacky. I play the drums. And this guy sitting next to me is Jet, our guitar player." Jet briefly makes eye contact. "And at the end of the table is our bassist, Raven." Raven nods. "And you already know Rage. We're USH. Do you know what that stands for?"

I'm guessing it stands for Untalented Shit Heads? I clear my throat. "Of course I do. United Sons of Hell. It's a great name." I bite my lip hard. "So, are you guys working on anything new?"

"We're always working on new songs, man," Rage chimes in. "Music is our life. What about you? Have you ever played live before, or are you a basement rockstar?"

I chuckle to myself. "I'm definitely not in the same league as Jet. I can promise you that. I just do the odd session job."

"Oh, really?" Jet straightens up, a challenge in his eyes. "You're a session player, are you? What albums have you played on?"

"Geez, lots, I guess. I was over in Zurich for a year, working on several different projects."

Everyone stops talking and stares at me. Then Jet stands up. "I've got to cut out early. I promised this little tighty that I'd pay her a visit tonight. I'll see you guys at the house later."

Everyone nods. When Jet walks past me, I tell him it was nice to meet him, but he just scoffs and continues walking.

"Don't worry about him," the bassist, Raven, says. "He is just intimidated by you. He's a barely average player, and none of us really mesh with the guy."

Rage glares at Raven. "Shut up, man. That's no one else's business."

I want to change the subject, so I ask where and when they'll play next. Rage tells me they have a gig in a week on Water Street at the Fort Club, a new live venue that just opened downtown.

Raven gulps the last of his drink. "We should go and eat somewhere. I'm starving."

Both Rage and Blacky agree. We all finish our drinks and stand up to leave, and I put up a hand in farewell. "Well, it was nice meeting all of you. I'll do my best to be at your next show."

I'm turning to leave when Rage stops me. "Hey, Lance. Are you hungry?"

I shrug. "I could eat."

"Great. Come with us."

I feel I've spent more than enough time with these punks tonight, but I know if I'm going to get close to them, I've got to put in the time. "Okay. Thanks, man."

We drive to a pizza joint in Rage's beat-up old Bronco. Just on the short jaunt to the restaurant, it's easy to sense that he controls his bandmates like puppets. They listen to him when he tells them to shut up, and none challenge him on his opinions. At the hole-in-the-wall pizzeria, Rage orders first, then everyone else after him.

Small booths line the walls of the narrow room, with a picnic table and rickety chairs at the back. We all grab our slice of soggy, paper-thin pizza and head to the back to sit down. Rage sits next to me. "Hey, man. You should come to a bash we're having at the house on the weekend. It's going to be off the charts. I can guarantee it."

I look at my pizza, but can't eat a bite yet. "That sounds like a party I'd be a fool to miss. Whereabouts is it?"

"Just off of East 29th and Lonsdale. It's the house with a red door. You can't miss it." Food slops around in Rage's mouth as he speaks. "Come alone."

"Of course. Thanks for the invite."

As I gag down my piece of wet cardboard, I listen as they talk about bands I've never heard of. Trevor's Terror. The Jackknifes.

"Yeah, they cut themselves on stage because they're so passionate about their songs. It's pretty powerful." Rage shakes his head. "I think we should come up with a gimmick too, but something no one else has thought of before. Something that'll make our live shows stand out."

The more bizarre shit that spews out of their mouths, the more it feels like I've been transported to the Twilight Zone. I can't wait to be back in reality.

Once everyone has choked down their food, Rage stands up and looks down at me. "Thanks for the hang. I'd give you a ride to your place or even back to the bar, but I'm not in the mood, so you're on your own. Don't forget about the party, though." He slaps my shoulder, and I watch the guys leave the shop.

I shake my head and pull my cell from my pocket to call a cab. I can't wait to get home and step into a hot shower. I need to wash off the scuzz from being around these low-lifes.

* * *

The neighbourhood is dead quiet as I walk from the taxi to my front door, the silence only broken by the jingling of keys as I pull them from my pocket. Once inside, I kick off my shoes and flick on the hallway light. At that moment, I hear a dull moan come from the front room.

I freeze, then listen again for the sound, just in case I've imagined it. It's not long before I hear a weird scuffling.

I'm not alone. Someone is lurking in the living room.

My pulse races as I slowly make my way up the hall. As I approach the entrance to the front room, the same shuffling sound comes from the darkness. If it's a burglar and I catch him in the act, I'll unleash on him and end up beating the guy to a bloody pulp. If there's one thing that makes me crazy, it's thieves. Over the years I've had too much gear and instruments stolen from me. Even though, there's little value in Mom's house, it's the principle.

As quietly as possible, I step completely into the dark living room. I don't want to scare them off. Then, I slide my hand along the wall until I feel the light switch. After taking a deep, silent breath and preparing myself, I flick it on.

I can barely believe what I see. My mother is sleeping in the old recliner.

"Mom," I holler. "Wake up!"

She groggily turns her head to look at me. "Why are you yelling?"

"Forget why I'm yelling. Why are you here?"

"I live here."

"That's real cute. Why are you not at the hospital?"

"It got weird. They gave me drugs that made me dopey, then had people come in and speak to me about having an addiction."

I can't help but shake my head. "I hate to point out the obvious, but they gave you sedating drugs to prevent you from having severe withdrawals. And as far as therapists speaking to you about addiction, that's par for the course when you're seeking help for alcoholism."

"I wish you wouldn't speak to me this way. You should have more compassion for your mother."

I walk over and crouch down by her chair. "Mom, it's dangerous for you not to be medically monitored."

"Yes, son. I'm aware of that. But being in the hospital and having decisions made for me...I just couldn't take it."

"Okay, so you must have a plan for your recovery then. What is it?" My sarcasm flows easily.

Her eyes meet mine with annoyance. "Just because I'm not on board with the hospital's plan doesn't mean I haven't thought of an alternative method for getting better."

"Great. What is it?"

"I'm going to call a detox centre tomorrow morning and get my name on the waitlist."

"Fine. But what will you do about your withdrawals in the meantime?"

"They gave me pills when I signed myself out of the hospital. Plus, my body is still full of the drugs they made me take while I was there."

I stand and extend a hand to her. "Come. I'll help you get to bed."

As I walk Mom up the stairs, I can't help but feel a sense of impending doom, wondering how I'm going to keep Mom away from the booze while she waits for a bed in rehab. Not to mention, I now have an opening to get closer to the USH band. If I have to babysit Mom all day and night, it will seriously fuck up my plans.

After she sits on the side of the bed, I gently pull off her shoes. "Do you want to get changed into your nightgown?"

She shakes her head. "I'm too tired. Why? Were you going to change your old ma?"

"Not while I still have my eyesight. There's some shit you can't unsee."

She snickers. "Smart ass."

Once her head rests on the pillow, I cover her with the blanket, then lean down and kiss her forehead. "Night, Ma."

"Lance." I'm almost out the door when she calls after me. "I know I'm a mess, but please give me the benefit of the doubt. I will get into a place that will help me, and until then, I won't touch a drop of booze. I promise."

Her words are sincere. I don't know if it's because I want so badly to believe her or if it's the conviction of her tone, but I suddenly feel more at ease. "Good night, my little escape artist. I'll see you in the morning."

"I love you, my boy."

* * *

I'm awoken by myriad headlights shining through the window and illuminating the walls. I rub my eyes, then glance at the clock beside my bed. It's 5 AM. Who the hell is driving around in this quiet little cul-de-sac at this hour?

I get up and look out the window—a police cruiser parks in front of the house. Two officers get out of the car and head up our driveway.

What the hell is this about?

I quickly pull on my jeans and hurry downstairs, hoping to get there before they knock and disturb Mom. She needs to sleep as much as she can right now. Thankfully, I make it down the stairs and open the front door in time. Two young cops, who look like clones of each other, stand on the stoop.

"What can I do for you, officers?" I'm certain they have the wrong house.

One cop gestures over my shoulder. "Mind if we come in and speak with you?"

"Can I ask what this is about? My mother is sleeping. She hasn't been feeling well. If we could just speak here, that'd be great."

The cops glance at each other, then back at me. "Are you the son of Anne Campbell?"

"Yeah. I'm Lance Campbell. Why?"

"We're sorry to have to tell you this, but your mother was involved in an accident. Unfortunately, she didn't make it. We're very sorry."

At first, I'm speechless. Then a wave of anger hits me. "My mother is upstairs sleeping. She just got out of the hospital."

Then, I look around the men to the driveway, and my knees almost buckle when I don't see Mom's car.

As if my body moves in slow motion, I turn away from the cops and head upstairs to my mother's room. As I swing the door open and see the covers pulled back on the empty bed, my heart falls deep in my chest, and my body shakes. *This can't be happening.*

Somehow, I make my way back downstairs to the front door, where the cops are still standing. "She's not there."

One of the men hands me Mom's wallet. "We found an empty bottle of vodka on the floor of the car. Based on a couple of eyewitness reports, the car was swerving shortly before impact. Was your mother known to drink?"

I ignore their question. "Impact? What did she hit?"

"A pole on Marine Drive and Capilano. The power is still out."

"Where's my mother now?"

"After the coroner attended the scene, she was transported to the morgue."

The other cop clears his throat. "Lance, we realize this must be very difficult for you, but if you could just answer a couple of questions—"

"Like what?" My voice comes out in a bark.

"Was your mother a known drinker?"

"She was in the process of getting help."

The cop writes something on a small pad. "Do you know if she had consumed any alcohol before driving this morning?"

"I didn't even know she was driving. I put her to bed, then I went to my room and crashed."

"All right. We have one more question, for now. Would you like us to call Victim Services to have someone come out and talk with you? They have some wonderful people working—"

"No. No, thank you. And if you're done with your questions—for now—I'd like to be alone."

"We understand." One officer hands me his card. "Please reach out if there's anything we can do."

As soon as the door is closed, I slide down the wall to the floor and put my hands over my face. A shiver runs through my body, and I feel darkness growing inside me.

Memories flash through my mind like clips from a film—my mother dropping me off for my first day of school, then sitting outside and waiting for me until the bell rang; her doting over me when I got sick; our unspoken language, where a glance was all she and I needed to know the other's feelings. When I was thirteen and told my parents I wanted to be a musician, it was my mother who encouraged me. She even saved up to buy my first guitar, an old beat-up Norman she got at a pawn shop. Even though she'd turned into a mess since I'd been away, I still never considered the possibility of losing her.

I'm not sure what pushed her to drink in the middle of the night. She was still drunk on the meds from the hospital. Was it the pain of losing Hannah? Or was it the DTs creeping back? Whatever prompted her to go and get booze, the initial cause of her pain remains the same—if Hannah hadn't been drugged and raped by that band of fuckwads, the whole chain of events wouldn't have happened. Hannah wouldn't have gotten into dope, she wouldn't have died, and Mom wouldn't have spiraled out of control. When those sonofabitches stole my sister's soul, they didn't only end her life. They ended my mother's, too.

I'm not afraid of getting caught for what I plan to do. No one would give two shits about scum getting taken out, especially musicians who have gotten a bad rap because of pigs like USH. Every time there's abuse by the hand of a musician, it shines badly on the rest of us.

They've taken everything that ever mattered away from me. Now, it's my turn to take from them. I'll make them suffer one by one until they beg for mercy, and then I'll hurt them some more.

Chapter 5

Almost a week has passed since I got the news about my mother. I've only gone out once to speak with the coroner and collect my mom's belongings from the car. Other than that, I've been in a weird haze, not eating or sleeping much. The only reprieve I get from how shitty I feel is from playing guitar.

I had to unplug the phone to silence the incessant amount of calls pouring in. I don't want to talk to anyone. But I was forced to deal with a funeral home when making arrangements to cremate my mother. I could barely handle that. Now, I'm told there's a whole list of things I'll have to do to close out my mom's bank account and contact the government to let them know she is deceased. They sure don't make it easy for grieving family members. There's so much bureaucratic bullshit to take care of, and everything needs to be done yesterday. It's sick.

I stare at the pictures of my family on the mantel, feeling detached and calloused. If I sit here for much longer, I'll go mindless.

I lumber into the kitchen and force down a half dozen crackers with cheese. Even though I have no motivation right now, I decide to go through the overwhelming amount of boxes and bins in the garage.

I'll have to sell the house soon. I definitely can't afford to pay the mortgage. Even if I could, there's no way in hell I'd want to live here now that my family is gone. I'd go mad.

I spend some time taking boxes from the garage into the kitchen and then start going through them. The first box I open contains old school ribbons and track and field trophies of Hannah's. She was so good at everything she did.

The next bin holds old Halloween decorations and costume remnants. I rummage through the items, then stop when I find an old rubber mask of a pig's head that I've never seen before. Hannah must've bought it for a theme party or something. I slide it over my head and look at my reflection in the garage door window. I look gruesome. It's definitely a mask that would scare little trick-or-treaters.

I pull it off my head and throw it on the kitchen floor, then continue sorting through the mountains of unnecessary items my mother refused to throw away or donate. Hannah and I used to jokingly call her a hoarder, which earned us a long lecture on the value of things, and why you shouldn't be so quick to throw stuff out. I flip open the lid of a smaller bin to find scads of old, cracked, and stained Tupperware. I shake my head with a laugh. "Yep, there's a ton of valuables here, Ma."

I'm lifting a box from the top of a heap when I hear my phone ringing in the front room. Even though I haven't answered calls, I know I should start. It could be the funeral home, again trying to arrange the pickup of Mom's ashes, something I've dreaded to do. It seems like no time has passed since I was at Hannah's funeral, watching her remains get lowered into the ground. Now I have to pick up an urn containing whatever's left of my mother.

As much as I yearn for even one tear to fall from my eyes, just to expel some of the pain, nothing comes.

I almost trip on the evil pig mask on my way to the living room. Kicking it out of my way, I sprint across the front room and grab my phone. "Hello?"

"Hey, dude, it's Reg."

"Oh. Hey, Reg."

"I haven't heard from you. Thought maybe you had enough of this place and headed back to Zurich."

"No. I'm still here. My mom was in a bad car accident a week ago. I've been climbing the walls and slowly losing my mind."

"What? Are you serious? Is she okay?"

"No. She took out a power pole on Marine Drive. From what the coroner said, she—"

"Coroner? She didn't make it?"

"No."

"What the hell? Lance. You should've called me. I would've been there for you. I'm so sorry, man. I loved Anne. She was great."

"To be honest, I didn't call anyone. I was too busy trying to keep from going insane."

"I'm coming over."

"No. I'm not really into having any—"

There's a click on the line as Reg hangs up.

"Shit!" I chuck my phone on the chair. The last thing I want to do is see anyone, but I know there's no point calling him back. Nothing dissuades him, not when his mind is set. He's like my mother in that way.

I amble up the stairs to my room to change. I've been wearing the same sweatpants for almost a week.

* * *

By the time I hear Reg's car in the driveway, I've tidied the living room as best I can. As I head for the door, I realize the pig's head is still on the floor next to the wall, where I'd kicked it earlier. With no place for it that doesn't look weird, I hurriedly toss the mask under the kitchen sink on my way to the door, which I open just as Reg is about to knock.

He's carrying a six-pack of beer in one hand and a large pizza in the other. "How are you doin', man?" His tone is laced with sympathy.

I shrug. "I'm getting by." I close the door behind him, and we go to the living room.

Reg sets the pizza down and cracks us both a beer. "I'm so sorry, man. I can't believe everything you're going through."

"Yeah, I'm finding it a little surreal myself."

He talks a bit about fond memories he has of my mom, but with only forced responses from me, the room soon gets an awkward vibe. I feel frustrated. I'd told him I wasn't in a good head space for company, but he came over anyway. Now, we're both uncomfortable.

I grab the remote and am just about to turn on the TV when Reg pipes up, "Hey, guess who's playing in Seattle in a few days?"

I'm relieved he'd changed the subject from Mom. "No idea."

"Roxanne. Their latest album is so good. It's beyond words. Have you heard any of their new tracks?"

I shake my head. "I've been a little preoccupied."

"I know, man. You're walking through a nightmare right now."

"It is what it is. There's nothing I can do to change it."

Reg tries, again, to distract me. "Anyways, I figured if you weren't doing anything in the next few days, maybe we should go see them. We can take my car."

"We would have to. I'm completely without wheels now."

"I guess that's right, you are."

"I'll probably pick up an old beater to boot around in. At least until I know what will happen with this house."

"Well, I have a suggestion. Why don't you save your cash and borrow my bike?"

"What, your old Yammy? You still got that thing?" I laugh.

"Yep. It's coming up on ten years since I bought it, and it was old then."

"Didn't you have a ton of carburetor issues with that thing?"

"And clutch issues. Not to mention the gas tank rusted from the inside out."

"Well, I can't afford to be picky. I appreciate the offer, Reg. I'll take you up on it, at least for now."

Reg tells me he'll crash here tonight, then take me to pick up the bike in the morning. By the time midnight rolls around, we've consumed all the pizza and beer, and I'm wiped out.

I grab a blanket and pillow for Reg from the closet. I asked him if he wants to crash in Mom's room, but barely get the question out.

He answers with, "No way, man." He asks where he should put the empty beer bottles, and I tell him to set them in the cupboard under the sink.

I go upstairs, and just when I enter my room, he bellows, "What the *hell*, man?"

I stick my head out my door. "Problems?"

Reg laughs. "I just about had a bloody heart attack when I opened the cupboard door and saw that freaky mask looking back at me. For a moment there, I thought you'd killed a pig."

Nope. Not yet, I haven't.

* * *

The morning is still and silent. I lie in bed, staring at the ceiling and listening to my breathing. I attempt to focus on what I need to do today, but my mind swirls like a cyclone, making it impossible to concentrate.

Maybe I'm going crazy. What if losing my baby sister and mother so close together made my brain snap? For the past week, especially, I've felt detached from myself. Like I'm observing my body from the outside. Nothing seems real. Most of the time, it's like I'm a robot going through the motions.

I get up when I hear noises coming from downstairs. When I open my bedroom door, a strong waft of coffee hits me.

In the kitchen, Reg is pouring two cups of coffee.

"What's up, Reg? How was the couch last night?"

"Manageable. Though, I appreciate my own bed a little more." He opens the fridge and grabs a liter of milk. After twisting off the top, he smells it and immediately grimaces. "Dude. This shit is nasty."

"I haven't been shopping for a while. It's probably best not to use anything in the fridge."

"Duly noted."

* * *

Reg pulls up the garage door. There, sitting in the middle of the room with nothing else around it, is the 1980 RD350 rusted and beaten Yamaha. Reggie's face glows with pride.

"Dude, I can't believe you still have this beast."

He laughs. "Watch what you say in her presence. This bike has gotten me out of some pretty sticky situations back in the day."

"I remember. All those beach parties we'd go to where the cops showed up. Everyone else drove in with their hot rods and couldn't make a fast escape, but we always got away on the bike."

"That's why I haven't gotten rid of her. Too many awesome memories." Reg pulls a key from his pocket and tosses it to me. "Make sure you keep the oil topped up. It's a two-stroke."

"I'll take care of her. Don't worry—I'll probably only drive at night when there's no one around."

Reg's expression turns confused. "Why is that?"

"Well, just look at the thing."

"You're a funny guy, Lance."

I push the bike out of the garage and kick it over. There's a loud bang, and a big plume of smoke shoots out the back end. I cough and wave my hand in front of my face. "Sweet ride. She purrs like a kitten."

Reg shakes his head, then hands me a helmet. "I'll touch base later."

* * *

The first main road I come to is Lonsdale Ave. Sitting at the red light, I remember what that little puke, Rage, had said about where he lived. *"Just off of East 29th and Lonsdale. It's the house with a red door. You can't miss it."*

I quickly signal to the right, and when the light changes, I head up the road toward Rage's place.

Of course, the moron didn't specify which way to turn on 29th, so I take my chances and turn left. After slowly riding past three older houses, I spot a shack-like structure with a red door and a trash-covered brown lawn.

So, this is where the rodents live.

I take a hard breath, realizing it's also where they raped Hannah and shattered her for the rest of her short life.

I visualize ramming the front door with the bike. Watching how fast the rats scatter before I find every one of them and then rip their throats out with my bare hands.

But this isn't a movie. This is real life. If I'm going to be successful in getting revenge for my sister, I've got to keep a cool head and strategize.

* * *

I motor slowly up our cul-de-sac. The smells of freshly cut grass and the joyful sounds of children playing fill the air. I park in the driveway, take off my helmet, and head to the house when I notice the old man next door. He's watering a flowerbed, but when his eyes meet mine, he frowns and waves. It's then obvious he's heard about what happened to Mom. I speed up in case he gets the urge to stop his watering to talk to me.

Safely inside and away from people, I flop down in the La-Z-Boy and assess what I know about USH.

They like young, innocent girls that they drug and then rape.

They live in squalor just up Lonsdale Ave.

Finally, all of them follow Rage's lead, except the guitar player, Jet, with whom none seem to have a strong allegiance.

I tap my finger on the armrest and think hard. Jet plays guitar, as do I, likely a lot better. If Jet is taken out of the band, and I convince the boneheads to let me fill his spot, I'll get close to the band. I can earn their trust, making each of them vulnerable and accessible. All I have to do is to take care of Jet.

My cell buzzes, and I look at the screen. It's a message from Reg.

"Hey, buddy. I went ahead and bought tickets to the Roxanne show in Seattle. Don't be pissed. You deserve to get away for a day. Talk later."

I sigh. As much as I live for music—particularly kick-ass bands like Roxanne—I have no time or headspace for a road trip. Though, I know I can't say no to Reggie. He's gone over and above to be supportive. So, I text back, *"You suck,"* then add a thumbs-up emoji.

For the next few hours, I return phone calls, tidy up the place, and head to the funeral home to pick up Mom's ashes, which, after returning home, I set on the mantel beside Dad and Hannah's pictures.

I decide to continue cleaning while I'm on a roll, so I grab a garbage pail and empty out all the expired items in the fridge. When I'm finished, I search the drawers and cupboards for twist-ties, eventually finding some under the kitchen sink. I'm about to close the cupboard door when I spot the pig's head mask. I grab it and a sharp butcher's knife from the drawer, then go to the front room. My backpack hangs on a peg, and I stuff the items inside with no set plan for how I'll use them.

As I'm coming inside after taking out the bag of spoiled food, a realtor calls regarding a message I'd apparently left a few days ago about selling the house. I don't even remember making the call. Nevertheless, I make an appointment for her to come and look at the place next week. Although I can't legally sell the house until all the bureaucratic bullshit is wrapped up, at least this woman can provide some insight into what must be done before the house hits the market.

* * *

It's 10 PM, and the hunger pains are finally annoying enough to force me out of the house. I toss my wallet in my backpack, grab the helmet, and head out.

Everything near my house is closed this time of night, so I drive down to Lonsdale, where a chicken hut is still open. I opt to eat inside the small joint, as I don't want to try and pack the food home on the bike. As I dip into my two-piece drumstick combo with coleslaw, a handful of young girls around Hannah's age walk in. They're giggling and locked into a language that only makes sense to them as the poor old guy behind the counter tries to take their order. Then they start taking selfies, even recruiting the guy behind the counter to participate in a few shots.

My first thought is that Hannah would have never behaved so silly in public. Then I remember that I had been away for a long time. Hannah could've changed a lot while I was overseas. She could—and likely had—acted with the same goofiness as these girls.

After eating, I toss my empty container in the garbage and head out. As the door to the eatery closes behind me, I still hear the squawking and laughter of the girls inside. *I really miss you, Hannah.*

Since it's late, I won't be as visible in the dark, and I decide to ride by the USH band's rundown house.

When I turn onto 29th Street, I spot a group of people converging on the front lawn of the house. From the look of the riffraff, scantily dressed young women, and a handful of goth-type males, it looks like the aftermath of a house party.

I ride past the place and pull into a small alleyway between two houses. I park in the shadows, then get off the bike and stand silently at the mouth of the alley, watching and listening.

A couple of partygoers walk past, only feet from where I'm hidden in the darkness. They're loud and obnoxious, shouting profanities and staggering up the street. A while later, a couple of the band members appear in front of the red door. It looks like Rage and Jet, and by their defensive stances, they seem at odds. I try to make out what they're saying, but they're too far away.

After a minute, Rage returns inside, and Jet raises his hand in a one-finger salute before walking down the stairs. When he turns in my direction, adrenaline rushes through me.

He trips once as he makes his way up the road. Once he's in earshot, I make out the words *"Mutherfuckers"* and *"They're nothing without me."* My heart pounds as he gets close enough that I hear his shiny black boots on the pavement.

I didn't plan on confronting him when I left the house tonight. But now I'm here, and he's here, and there's no one else around. I grab my backpack and reach inside for the knife. In the process, my hand touches the rubber pig's head. I quickly set the knife on the bike seat, slip the mask on, and then grab my weapon.

He's only feet away from me now. *What should I do?*

The answer becomes clear when I picture my baby sister lying drugged on a bed, this putrid waste of skin grunting on top of her. Without thinking, I call out his name. "Jet."

He sways to a stop and looks around. "Who the fuck is that?"

I blurt out the first words that come to mind. "Do you have a light?"

"Where are you, man? I can't see you."

I take a step into the half-light, exposing only my face.

"Ha. You're a pig." He's teetering on his feet. "That's hilarious."

"Are you going to give me a light or not?"

"Yeah, yeah, pig man. Just a second." With drunken clumsiness, he fumbles for a lighter until finding one in his synthetic coat pocket. With a wavering hand, he reaches the lighter toward me.

Like a snake, I strike fast. My hand latches onto his wrist, and I yank him into the darkness.

"What the fuck, man?" he shrieks.

I push my mouth against his head. "You revolting little prick. You ruined my life. Now, I will hurt you the same way you hurt my sister."

"I don't know what the hell you're talking about. Let me go." His voice is high, and he seems to be quickly sobering up. Whatever I'm going to do, I'd better do it quickly, or someone will hear him.

I tighten my grip on the knife. "You made a mistake the day you laid your hands on Hannah. I should cut your fucking fingers off."

"No. I'm a guitar player. Not my fingers."

"Not your fingers? How about not my sister?"

The first plunge of the blade happens without warning. It's like my hand acted alone. But when Jet chokes out a scream and tries to pull away, I drive the blade deeper into his gut with full intention. After about five hard thrusts, his shrieks become gurgles.

Out of breath, I release him. He falls to the ground, limp and lifeless. I quickly retreat into the darkness as a wave of nausea rises from my gut. I bend over and puke up the chicken combo meal I had earlier.

When my stomach empties, I straighten up and take a few deep breaths. *This is crazy. What the hell just happened?*

There is no way I foresaw any of this happening tonight. When I think about the knife, and how many times I drove it into him, I feel queasy again. Then I remember why I came here in the first place—vengeance for Hannah. My queasiness fades quickly, and a grin cracks my face. "That's one down, little sis. Three to go."

I quickly stuff the mask into my pack, along with the bloodied knife. Then I jump on the bike and slide on the helmet. Funny enough, my hands aren't shaking, and I'm breathing with ease.

I ride straight home. I know I've got to get rid of the evidence quickly. After I park the bike, I hurry into the house, hoping no one is watching from any of the neighbouring houses.

When I take my pack off to hang it up, I catch a glimpse of my face in the hallway mirror. There's a wide smear of blood on my neck. I look down at my hands and see that both palms are covered in blood. It feels so surreal. I actually took someone's life tonight. The life of a dangerous lowlife who prayed on innocent girls, but a life nevertheless. I should feel some level of remorse.

But I don't. I feel proud of what I've done. Not only have I wiped out a predator, but I've also taken the first step at vindicating musicians everywhere. I'm so sick of hearing about piece of shit band guys who commit heinous crimes that shine badly on the rest of us musicians. It's been that way for decades. A freak will do something disgusting, and the whole industry gets put on trial. Legitimate artists shouldn't have to bear the dishonour of a few scumbags.

I go upstairs to the bathroom to wash the blood off my neck and hands. Then I glance down at my clothes. There are splatters of blood all over me.

I wasn't expecting this. I've watched enough cop shows to know that one speck of blood found on me or in my house would seal my fate. I don't want to go to jail. I wouldn't last a day in the joint. Besides, I can't imagine being penalized for what I did. I should be honoured for wiping out a person who would have undoubtedly caused more hurt.

I slip off my jeans and shirt and roll them into a ball. After donning a pair of shorts and another shirt, I go downstairs, grab the mask and canvas backpack, and hurry into the front room. There, I open the fireplace flue and toss the items onto the empty log grate. I search around the house until I find a small container of lighter fluid, then douse the pants before tossing in a lit match.

Everything burns slowly, and I become entranced by the yellow flames. I can't believe how significantly my life has changed in such a short time. It seems like only yesterday I was in Zurich, in the studio, laying down awesome tracks with a team of great musicians. I was completely in my element. Now, I've lost my mother and baby sister, and I'm sitting in front of a fire, completely alone, burning evidence from the murder I just committed. Life sure has a fucked-up sense of humour.

After the mask, clothes, and bag burn to ash, I turn out the lights and head to bed. Right before I pass out, I check my phone. There are three messages from Reg. In each one, he mentions the same thing—the concert in Seattle and how stoked he is that we're going.

I set the phone on my nightstand and close my eyes. For the first time in a long time, I'm relaxed and calm enough to sleep.

Chapter 6

A loud knocking at the front door wakes me. I roll over and glance at the clock. It's 9 AM. Who the hell is at the door so early?

Half asleep, I get downstairs to the foyer and look through the small window. It's Reggie. When I open the door, he holds out two sparkplugs. "Here. I forgot to give these to you. You may need them for the bike."

"I can't believe you came over so early. I was sleeping like a rock."

"I'm sorry, man. I thought I'd drop them off before work."

I nod and take the plugs from him. "Okay. Cool. I'm going to go and jump in the shower."

Reg turns to leave, then stops and looks back at me. "Did you go out last night?"

"Briefly. I went out for food, then came straight home." Suddenly, I feel nervous. "Why?"

Reg's eyes are wide. "Some guy got stabbed just off of Lonsdale. Apparently, there were cop cars and emergency vehicles for blocks, a real circus. Crazy shit."

"How did you find out a guy got stabbed?"

"My neighbour's daughter lives beside the alleyway where they found the guy."

I shrug. "It was probably drug-related. It usually is."

Reg says he'll text me later, then reminds me about the Seattle concert. "I hope your passport is up to date."

"Yes, Mommy. I've got everything I need."

After Reg drives away, I jump into the shower and get dressed, figuring I'd drive out to grab a coffee somewhere. Outside, I slide on the helmet and am about to climb on the motorcycle when I notice reddish-brown spots on the side of the tank. I quickly lean down for a closer look. The marks are a lot like dried blood.

Forgoing the coffee, I head straight to Marine Drive to the self-serve car wash. I go through about twenty bucks in tokens, meticulously scrubbing every inch of the old Yamaha.

Satisfied there's no more evidence to link the bike or me to the stabbing, I ride to the nearest café for a much-earned coffee. Afterward, I head home and set my focus on the knife and where to hide it. I think in front of the TV for a while until an ad comes on for white water rafting, and I smile.

After squeezing my hands into a pair of my mother's gardening gloves, I wrap layers of paper towel around the blade and handle of the knife. I stick the knife into my waistband before donning a longer windbreaker that covers the front of my jeans.

Once on the bike, I head onto Highway 1 East, then take the turn-off to Maple Ridge. Thankfully, the traffic isn't too bad. Once I see the Fraser River, I keep driving until I find a spot where nobody is around.

I park in a grassy area, then get off the bike and casually walk down to the riverbank. I look around, then slide the knife out of my jeans. I'm just about to unwrap it when out of the bush springs a yellow retriever.

The dog stops, scans me a couple of times, then runs past me. I tuck the blade under my windbreaker, my heart pounding. My concern isn't the animal but whoever may be following behind it. I stand quietly for a while, listening for the sound of feet crunching through the brush. After about fifteen minutes of hearing nothing, I inch forward until my feet almost touch the water, then quickly uncover the blade. After one final look around, I fling the knife into the turbulent river.

Happy with where it landed, I turn around and about yell when I see an old man standing behind me. Caught off-guard, I can only stare at him.

Finally, he breaks the silence. "You see a yellow dog come past?"

I point in the direction I last saw the retriever, and the man nods before walking away.

I hurry back to the bike. As I swing my leg over the seat, I wonder how long the old guy had been standing there. I wonder if he saw me toss the knife.

For the remainder of the evening, I do my best to distract myself from worrying about the old man. I order a pizza and listen to my father's old Herb Alpert and the Tijuana Brass albums. As I'm going to bed around midnight, Reg texts. *"See ya tomorrow, buddy. I'll pick you up at 5 PM sharp. Make sure you have your passport and your I.D. I wouldn't want to go without you."*

* * *

As the glow of morning floods the room, I look out the window at the cul-de-sac, at the well-maintained older homes with their perfectly manicured lawns and flower beds. My parents used to have the respect of every resident in the neighbourhood. That is until my father died. After that, Mom, Hannah, and I lived under the watchful eye of every nosey parker that lived within viewing distance of our front door. I can only imagine the gossip floating around about Hannah's death and now my mother's. I guess that's why it doesn't feel like home to me anymore—all the judgemental energy floating around. As I move forward with my plan of wiping out USH, I'll be cautious when

I come home. There are eyes always watching.

I spend the day going through Mom's closet, looking through her personal papers and photo albums of my parents when they first got married. They looked so young and hopeful, oblivious to the shit show that would unfold years later.

By the time Reg shows up, I'm ready to get out of the house and leave behind my depressing trip down memory lane.

* * *

Golden fields of hay line both sides of the narrow road as we head south. About twenty minutes before we reach the border, the traffic stops. Reg drums his fingers impatiently on the wheel. "Shit, look at the lineup to get into the States. I'm going to be pissed if the concert starts without us."

"Just throw on some tunes and kick back. It's not like we can do much about it."

Reg reaches into the console and pulls out a CD. *Rescue You*, by Joe Lynn Turner, his solo album from 1985. There's a killer fill at the beginning with a reverse delay that rocks.

Reg and I both tap to the beat of the title song. Joe Lynn has such a soulful delivery and an unmatchable talent. With his notable contributions to Rainbow, Deep Purple, and Yngwie Malmsteen's band, his vocals can't be beat. Some of the studio musicians I've worked with have seen him perform live, and they all say the same thing—Joe Lynn Turner is, bar none, one of the best vocalists of our time.

We finally get to the venue—a legendary arena that has hosted countless epic rock concerts. After twenty minutes of parking fuckery, we get to the wicket booth, where Reg pulls out the tickets and hands them to a cute but indifferent looking blonde.

Inside, almost every seat is taken. Ours are two lone empties off to the left of the F.O.H area. Reg and I squeeze into the chairs, which look tiny between the two portly men on either side of us.

As we wait for the show to start, I look up on the stage to check out the band's gear, like the amps and the drums. Off to the side is the monitor desk, where a guy with a ponytail tweaks knobs on the mixing board as he gets things ready.

Reg stands. "I'm going to get a drink. Do you want one?"

I give him a thumbs-up.

As soon as Reg leaves, the guy next to me starts talking loudly to his friend about how he has the band's first album from 1988 and how he saw them on the Late Show that same year when they performed Play That Funky Music. The guy is obviously stoked to be here—we all are—but I swear, if he keeps chattering through the whole concert, my boot is going straight up his ass.

Reg makes it back just as the intro starts. He passes me a plastic cup of Coke and grins. I can tell he's happy to be here. Both of us have been devout Roxanne fans since I can remember.

When the house lights go down, everyone screams with anticipation. Then, the band walks on stage, and the crowd is on their feet.

"Keep On Keepin' On" is the first song they break into, a newer tune that kicks ass and proves that the band still has all the ingredients to maintain the title as one of the best rock and roll groups out there. Song after song, Roxanne sustains the same high energy level, with Jamie Brown blowing us away with incredible vocals, stopping only long enough to shout out a few words to the screaming crowd. When the lead guitarist, John Butler, does a wicked solo, Reg and I smile at each other and shake our heads—the guy is on fire.

After the concert ends, I feel like I'm high as a kite as we filter out amidst the throngs of people. Reg gets swallowed up by the crowd for a few minutes, then resurfaces just past the entrance doors outside.

He shakes his head as we start our long journey to the car. "They were fucking flawless, man."

"I know. I feel like tossing my guitar in the trash after watching Butler play."

Reg chuckles. "Tell me about it. Did you hear how deadly Joe Infante performed? The guy has killer skills but doesn't overplay. He sits perfectly in the pocket with David Landry."

"Yeah, I agree. And man, Landry was on his game. That guy has so much confidence and power. Great meter, too." I let out a huge breath. "That was by far the best concert I have been to in ages. I'm glad I came." For the first time in a while, I'm not thinking about Hannah, Mom, or USH. I feel lighter.

After navigating through Seattle, we get on-route to the border, stopping once to grab burgers at a drive-thru and to fill up on gas. Once we're stuck again in a long line of border traffic, Reg asks if I plan on returning to Europe.

I shake my head. "Not yet. Too much unfinished business to take care of here first."

"You must miss playing, though."

"Of course I do. It's the only thing that makes sense to me."

Reg turns on a Seattle rock station that plays the best of AOR. After a few songs, the announcer breaks in with entertainment news. The headline story is about a Toronto-based pop group that has achieved minimal success. Two members are apparently up on charges of sexually assaulting a minor.

Immediately, a powerful rage bubbles in the pit of my gut. I reach over and turn off the radio.

"Dude, what did you do that for? I was listening to that."

"I can't do it, man. I don't want to hear about young girls getting abused and destroyed by entertainers. It makes me crazy."

Reg is taken aback by my outburst. After a few beats, he speaks again, his voice low and calming. "Don't worry, man. The bastards have been caught. I'm sure they'll be going away for a long time."

I shake my head with a harsh laugh. "You think so? I don't. I predict these little pukes will get off with a slap on the wrist. Maybe have to pay a hefty fine."

"Oh, come on, Lance. They aren't going to let these guys walk. They abused a minor."

I laugh again. "It's great you have such deep faith in the system, Reg. But you're not being realistic. The jails and court rosters are full. Even if criminals get charged, it doesn't mean they'll get what they deserve."

Reggie lets out a sigh. "I know a lot of cops who work hard to seek out bad guys. I know for sure they do their best to—"

"It's not the cops who are keeping predators out of jail. It's the system."

Abandoning his initial plan of calming me down, Reg amps up his energy to meet mine. "What are you suggesting, then? How should these guys be dealt with?"

"Brutally. They should have to face the ultimate punishment for destroying someone's life. An eye for an eye."

"Define brutally."

"They should be taken out to a field and shot in the head like a sick animal."

"You don't mean that."

"You'd be surprised."

There's a concern in Reg's eyes. "Why are you so enraged by this? It's not like you've ever had to deal with this stuff. No one you know has been assaulted."

"Wrong."

"Who? Who do you know that got assaulted?"

I don't reply.

Reg taps on the steering wheel and keeps his eyes on the road. Then, suddenly, he looks over at me. "Your sister? Was Hannah assaulted?"

I turn my head and look out the window.

Next thing I know, Reg is pulling to the side of the road. The car stops and Reg turns to face me fully. "Lance, what the fuck? Tell me. Did someone take advantage of your kid sister?"

"Yep." I stare hard out the window.

"Buddy, I am so sorry. Why the hell didn't you tell me? I could've been there for you."

"I don't, now nor then, need anyone to be there for me. I'm dealing with it."

"Was Hannah okay? I hope to God she wasn't hurt too badly—"

"No. She wasn't okay. It affected her so badly that she got into drugs—you know how that ended. The assault also took out Mom, who couldn't deal with losing Hannah. She got trapped in a bottle of vodka until that car crash freed her."

Reg puts a hand on my shoulder. "I'm so sorry, man. I knew Hannah died from an overdose. I just never knew why." He pauses. "Can I ask you one more thing, and then we'll change the subject?"

I make eye contact with him. "What?"

"Before, you mentioned you were dealing with it. What did you mean by that?"

"What are you worried about?"

"I'm concerned you're thinking ways you shouldn't be thinking. Seeking revenge, vigilante-style. I hope to hell that I'm way off on this. I would hate to see you get yourself into trouble."

I force my tone to be light. "No worries, man. It's all good. It's not like I'm going on a killing spree or anything. You know me, Reg, I'm a peaceful guy."

After a few moments, Reg shrugs and laughs. "You're right. Sorry, Lance. I don't know what I was thinking."

* * *

Once we're back in the neighbourhood, Reg suggests we go to Lulu's for a drink. I agree, but I regret it once we arrive. Had I remembered the loud canned music in this place, I would've suggested we go somewhere else. It would be tolerable if they played good tunes, but this techno sub-heavy shit gives me an instant headache.

I rub my temple and lean close to Reg. "Whoever's the maestro in control of the tunes should be shot." Reg snorts and shakes his head.

After we get our beers, we spend the next hour trying to chat over the music. By the end of round two, we've had enough of the racket and agree to leave.

On our way to the car, Reg searches for his keys but can't find them. He goes back inside the club to see if he left them at the bar while I wait outside. A moment later, I see three goth-like dudes walking toward the entrance. It's not until they're under the neon lights that I recognize them. It's USH— all except for the guitar player.

As Rage lifts his eyes and recognizes me, I wave and call a greeting.

"Oh, hey, man." His voice is low.

I can tell the three aren't their usual upbeat, obnoxious selves, and I can guess why. "You're missing one." I can't keep the smile off my face.

"Our guitar player was murdered."

"Wow, how bad was he?"

The three look at me with disgust. "Not cool, man," Blacky barks. "Jet is lying in a freezer at the morgue, and you're cracking jokes."

I arrange my face into an expression of shock. "Oh. Were you serious? I had no idea. I thought you were yanking my chain."

Raven looks on the edge of tears. "He was gutted like a pig."

You mean, by a pig. "That's awful. Do they know who did it?" Inside, I'm grinning to beat hell.

Rage shakes his head. "Not yet. Jet rubbed a lot of people the wrong way, but he didn't deserve what happened to him."

Wanna bet? "I feel terrible for you guys. I don't know what else to say."

"Thanks, man. We're gonna go on a bender tonight. Tomorrow, we've got to figure out how to keep the band going."

"I guess that's right. You're without a guitar player now."

Rage nods. "And we have a gig coming up, too."

"Geez. You're sure in a bad spot. Well, let me know if I can stand in for Jet until you find someone later. I learn songs pretty quickly."

Rage slowly nods as if he's giving my offer some serious thought. He then pulls out his phone and passes it to me. "Here. Punch in your number. I'll think about it and call you tomorrow."

I'm just handing the cell back after inputting my digits when Reg comes out of the bar, dangling his keys. "Found 'em." Then he stops and tilts his head, obviously baffled as to why I'm hobnobbing with the vinyl-clad goth heads.

I look back at USH. "Okay, guys. I've got to go. Try and have a good night, and again, I'm sorry about Jet."

They nod, then head inside.

I turn toward Reg, who stares at me with his head still cocked. "Friends of yours?"

"I hope so." I'm smiling as I head for the car.

After we get in the car, Reg doesn't start it right away, instead looking at me with a bemused grin. "What the hell was that about?"

"Nothing. I just started talking to them while I was waiting for you. They may be looking for a guitar player."

Reg blinks in shock, then starts laughing hard, holding his stomach. "I'm pretty sure you don't fit into that lineup."

"You don't know that. The key to being a good musician is versatility."

"But goth music? Really?"

"I thought you liked all genres of music, Reg."

"I do, but *you* don't. And I'm sorry, man, but I can't see you wearing a black overcoat and tight plastic pants." He nudges me. "Are you going to get face piercings and smear on some pretty black lipstick, too?"

"Good idea, Reg. Maybe I'll get one of those nose hoops like bulls have. I'd be stylin'."

He smirks, then gets a serious look. "Tell me honestly. Are you really thinking of playing music with those guys or just messing with me?"

"Why? Do you think I'm losing it?"

"Not entirely. I think your tuning may be a bit off."

Once home, I thank Reg for taking me to the concert. "I'll text you tomorrow."

He nods, and I get out of the car. I can feel the watchful eyes of the neighbourhood looky-loos as I head into the house.

After grabbing a tall glass of water, I sit in the La-Z-Boy and smile at the empty fireplace. What a night—I see a wicked concert, then run into those little pukes by a stroke of pure luck. All in all, I'd say it was a pretty good night.

After about twenty minutes, I go to bed and lie awake for half the night, reliving and reveling in how upset Jet's bandmates were over his death. So far, everything is going according to plan. I must be patient and bide my time so I don't fuck up. Regardless of how well the Jet thing played out, I must be more careful next time. A single slip-up could cause everything to go to shit.

I know I require sleep, so I close my eyes and try to calm down. Images of Mom and Hannah float through my mind as I drift off.

* * *

A loud clanging sound, like metal hitting cement, wakes me from a deep sleep. I quickly jump out of bed and look out the window to see a woman in a tight blue tracksuit and ponytail bending over to pick up a realtor's sign she'd accidentally dropped on the sidewalk.

I remember Dad's face whenever he saw a realtor coming to the house. The edges of his mouth would drop, and a severe line would appear between his brows. *"How many damn times do I have to tell these people we're not interested in selling! They're like flies swarming around a picnic."*

I quickly grab my cell phone and check my messages. There's a text from a realtor saying she'll be in the area and wants to speak with me. What a crock of shit. She probably drove in from the Fraser Valley or someplace. I respect that times are tough, especially in sales, but she could have at least waited for my reply before deciding to land on my doorstep.

She glances up at my window, and I quickly move out of sight. I'll wait her out. Regardless of how determined she is, when I don't answer the door, I'm hoping she'll eventually give up and go away.

After fifteen long minutes of repeated knocks on the front door and me staying as quiet as possible, I get frustrated. I feel like a little animal hiding in a burrow while a hungry predator lurks outside—it's ridiculous.

Finally, I hear the grumpy old neighbour from next door tell her that I'm not home and "There's no sense hanging around."

I peek out the window and watch as she lugs the awkward sign back to her car and struggles to get it into her trunk. Even though I'm annoyed, I'm also relieved knowing the house has gotten her attention. She obviously sees it as marketable.

Later that afternoon, my phone rings. I look at the screen but don't recognize the number. Usually, I wouldn't answer a call from a random number. Nothing pisses me off more than annoying spam calls, but I figure, *what the hell*, and answer, "Hello?"

"Hey, Lance. It's Rage. I want to discuss something with you."

I stand up straight. "Okay. Shoot."

"Me and the other guys in the band had a meeting, and we've decided to try you out as the new guitar player for USH." His tone suggests I just won the lottery.

I shake my head and quietly snicker. *I guess this is where I'm supposed to act thrilled and grateful.* "Wow, really? That is so cool. I haven't slept all night because I was excited, wondering if you would call." The lie sticks in the back of my throat, creating a dry lump.

"Just keep quiet until it's official. We still have to see how you play."

You moron. Keep it secret? Dude, I'll be embarrassed just playing with you guys— I'm not adding salt to the wound by telling anyone. "I totally get it. Don't worry, Rage. I'm just happy to be given the chance."

"After the whole Jet thing, we were going to wait for a while before we played again, but we know he wouldn't want us to miss any gigs. USH always comes first."

"Yeah, that's a great credo." *What a complete dipshit.*

"All right, give me your email, and I'll send you MP3s of our songs."

"Great. I can't wait to get them. I'll start learning the songs right away."

Rage informs me that their next gig is the day after tomorrow, so I should make sure I'm prepared. We say a quick goodbye, and I text him my email. I make a quick pot of coffee, then grab my guitar from the bedroom and turn on my laptop to wait for shithead's MP3s.

Reg texts, which helps pass the time. He wants to know about my schedule, as he's already got another concert in his scope. I swear, that guy spends all his money on instruments, new gear, and live shows. He's always been like that, even when we were young. Other kids would go camping or on vacation in the summer, but not Reg. Not if there was a concert coming to town that he wanted to see. I don't know how many shows he made his father take him to, but I'm guessing he's easily seen over a hundred by now.

I was just as focused on music, but my passion wasn't seeing tons of concerts. It couldn't be. My father was hard-pressed to shell out that much cash. Instead, I would play my guitar day in and day out. If I was forced to go on our yearly camping trip in a rented motorhome, I brought my guitar and played until I drove everyone nuts. It was a release for me and a way to express my feelings, which I always had issues with something. If I felt down, I'd play blues riffs, and if I were hyped up, I'd shred until my fingers bled.

I see a new message notification in my email. Rage has sent me the music. This should be interesting.

I open each file and save it to my desktop. After storing all seven files, I click on number one and turn up the volume.

The song starts with a strange, distorted sound. Then come the drums, which sound like someone falling down the stairs—no rhythm and sloppy. Next is the bass, which starts offbeat and is way too busy. As if it wasn't bad enough, Rage screams, "We are USH, and we want you to serve us."

I shake my head in disbelief. *How the hell does this ridiculous band ever get booked?*

Nothing makes sense about their music or their lyrics. It takes most of the night to learn the first three clusterfuck tunes. If the guys I worked with in the studio saw me strumming this garbage, they'd lose all respect for me. But dumbing down is a necessary evil, and I'll do whatever it takes to get in and gain their trust.

I crawl into bed at around 2 AM with a searing headache and sleep like a rock until the sawing sound of the neighbour's lawnmower wakes me. Knowing there's no chance of falling back to sleep with that racket, I get up and dress.

Downstairs, I make coffee and watch the local news to see if anything comes up about Jet, but there's no mention of the murder. I'm sure it's police protocol to keep things under wraps while they conduct their investigation. I smile, relieved that I took everything of mine home with me. Nothing ties me to the murder.

Murder. That's a strong word that I don't prefer. I don't feel like a murderer. more like an exterminator. If the police only knew what a slime bag Jet was, I'm sure they wouldn't give two shits about carrying out an investigation—at least not a thorough one.

I spend the rest of the day packing up my mother's room and loading the boxes into the garage. When the pain of her memory gets too much, I play guitar to distract myself.

Tomorrow night I play with the band of fuckwads. This will definitely be the low point of my career, and in public, no less. The only good thing about performing on the same stage as these fools is that it'll get me closer to them. It won't take long to earn their trust, and then I'll be in the best position to exact revenge.

* * *

A warm breeze flows over the Lionsgate Bridge as I ride toward downtown. I follow the line of traffic through Stanley Park, looking to the roadside and seeing garbage strewn all over the ground.

The park was always a destination spot for my family on the weekends. I remember walking past the colourful paintings at the artisan stands and smelling the intoxicating aroma from the fish and chip stand. My dad always ordered the battered cod with fresh-cut fries wrapped in newspaper. The four of us would sit on the grass under one of the tall Douglas firs and watch all the boats on the water. Then, on the way back to the car, Mom bought a bag of peanuts to feed the park squirrels. On one occasion, my dad decided to pet a baby squirrel—the little rodent grabbed my dad's thumb and sawed around it like a can opener. While at the hospital waiting for my dad to get stitches, I heard my mom mutter, "If brains were gold, he wouldn't have enough to fill a tooth."

I arrive at the building that houses the small, hole-in-the-wall bar. Inside, I walk down a hallway, where every wall is painted black with red skulls.

"Very classy," I scoff under my breath.

I follow green arrows that lead down two more hallways until I reach the bar door. On it is a sign: *"Enter at own risk."*

This is going to suck so badly. Just shoot me now.

When I push the door open, I am immediately drawn to the scads of empty tables. The only populated area is one long bench near the small bar, where ten black-clad twenty-year-olds gathered.

As I walk toward the postage stamp-sized stage, I glance over at the table. I've never seen so many silver hoops on people's faces. *At least they have the good style sense to offset all that metal with some nice black lipstick.* I smile and shake my head, then take my guitar off my back and lean against the stage to wait for USH, the stars of the shit show.

After a painful twenty minutes, the Three Stooges finally enter the room. All three looked like they had just spent all their government cheques at Hot Topic. Fishnet arm sleeves, ripped black tops, zipper wristbands, and a bunch of colourful weird shit tied around their necks. Obviously, they're trying to look younger to relate to their developmentally arrested fans, but this is ridiculous.

Rage saunters up to me. "I told you to dress up. You look like you're going shopping or something. You don't match the rest of us."

I'd rather drink bleach than wear any of your fucked up outfits. "Sorry, man. I bought a pair of those nifty plastic pants you're wearing, but when I got them home, I couldn't cram my ass into them."

Rage glares at me. "Whatever. So that you know, you look stupid being the only one not in stage clothes."

I'm willing to live with that shame.

Rage gestures to my throat. "At least take off that gold shit. We wear silver only."

At that moment, I want to turn right around and leave. Either that or throttle Rage's skinny neck right then and there. But this is a means to an end. Getting in close with the band is too important. So, I swallow my anger and take off Hannah's necklace.

Everyone starts setting up. Rage takes a small kit out of his pocket and sets it near the back of the stage. I nonchalantly walk over and glance down. It's an insulin kit.

Rage has diabetes. That's very interesting—a vulnerability—a big one.

I smile, thinking about the possibilities. With a guy that parties like him, it would be a perfectly logical conclusion that he accidentally gave himself the wrong dose. One big dosage could lead to his demise, and I would never have to worry about getting caught.

As for the other two, their biggest weakness is that they're complete morons. It's too bad stupidity isn't fatal, but I guess if it were, we'd have no politicians. The other bandmates' lack of awareness will make things much easier to manipulate into something deadly.

Once we're all plugged in and ready to go, Rage takes the mic. "All right, my little demons. We are United Sons of Hell, and we're going to rock your world."

What a fucking idiot. For a moment, I have visions of taking off my guitar and whacking him over the head with it.

As soon as we start to play, it's painfully obvious the drummer began with the wrong backing track. Rage starts to sing, and I grit my teeth. He's pitchy and screechy, like a cat with its tail caught under a rocking chair.

Ironically, the "fans" can't tell the difference. Instead of puking, covering their ears, and running out of the place, they all converge to the front of the stage. I'm back in the Twilight Zone as, song after ear-bleeding song, the gothy fans jump around and cheer.

When the last painful set ends, I quickly unplug my guitar and stuff it into my gig bag. I force myself to thank Rage for the incredible opportunity and am just about to escape when Rage hollers, "How did it feel playing with USH?"

Like having a root canal and a colonoscopy simultaneously.

* * *

Outside the bar, I stand beside the exit and shake my head. *Hannah, if you only knew the sacrifice I just made for you.*

I head toward the bike when I spot a hotdog stand on the corner of the street. The last thing I should be consuming is a nitrate stick, but since there's nothing quick to whip up at home, I throw caution to the wind, swing my gig bag over my shoulder, and walk over to join the line-up.

Four younger women stand directly in front of me, all laughing and unsteady on their feet. Immediately, I can tell it will be a long wait, and there's nothing more annoying than drunk people hollering incoherently and repeatedly banging into you.

Several unbearable minutes later, I'm about to give up and leave when someone taps me on the shoulder. I turn around and immediately lose my breath.

She's a young woman, somewhere in her early twenties. A vision of long, raven hair falling around a perfect face. She looks up at me with the most striking blue eyes I've ever seen. "Hi. Have you been waiting long?"

I open my mouth to answer, but nothing comes out. I shake my head.

She smiles, perceptively aware of her power. "Good. I'm starving."

I look around her but don't see anyone. She's here alone.

One of the women in front of me backs up and digs her heel into my foot. I'm about to say something when the goddess beside me puts her hand on the woman's back.

The drunkard whips around angrily. "Why the hell are you touching me?"

In a diplomatic tone, the raven-haired girl tells the drunk to watch where she's stepping. The swaggering female mutters something inaudible then turns her attention back to her friends.

I smile at the woman. "Thanks. I'm sure if I'd said something, it would've sparked a huge protest."

"Yeah." She winks. "You've got to be careful out here on the mean streets."

"True. They're probably normal people during the week, but as soon as the weekend comes, instant assholes. Just add alcohol."

The line starts to move quickly, and before I know it, it's my turn at the small counter. I order a fully loaded dog, then tell the guy that I'm paying for the woman behind me as well.

She overhears. "You don't have to buy mine."

"It's the least I can do after you saved my life."

I grab my hotdog and head to a side counter that holds different condiments. Once I'm done, I turn to find a place to stand and eat, but I almost bump into the dark-haired beauty.

She looks up at me and smiles. My hands start to tremble. "I thought," she says, "since you bought me food, the least I can do is eat with you."

I can't believe this is happening.

She points to a cement fixture that serves as a small fountain in the daytime. Thankfully, there's no water spouting and room to sit along the ledge.

We sit, and I turn to her. "What's your name?"

"Tessa. And yours?"

She so enamors me it takes me a second to answer, "Lance."

Tessa smiles. "Lancelot. I like it." She raises the hotdog to her mouth and takes a bite. The wiener looks pale and has green speckles in it.

"Hey, I don't think you should eat that. It looks off." I glance down at mine to make sure it doesn't look the same. Thankfully, it doesn't.

She finishes chewing and grimaces. "Yeah, it's a tofu dog. Not what I expected it to taste like."

"What a relief. I thought it was rotten. Are you a vegetarian?"

She shakes her head. "Not at all. I like to try new things."

I laugh. "And a tofu dog was on your list? What's it made out of, anyway? Soybean?"

"I think so. Though it tastes like wet Styrofoam."

I offer to get her another dog, but she declines. As we sit and talk, I learn she works at a late-night coffee bar on Denman Street. She used to be a ballet dancer but quit because of the politics. When she asks about my life, I give her the polished version and leave out all the dark details about Hannah and my mom. Throngs of rowdy people walk by, but I can only hear Tessa for some reason.

"So." She nudges my bag with her foot. "What's with the guitar?"

For a moment, I had forgotten about the shit show I had just played. "I was filling in as the guitar player for USH, a glam-goth band."

"USH?"

"Trust me. you don't want to know."

She smiles. "Well, if they're a crappy band, why did you play with them?"

I shrug. "Maybe for a lesson in humility."

She laughs. "I'm sure they aren't so terrible."

"No. Trust me. I would rather play a polka fest than fill in with this band again. And yet, this band managed to get a paying gig. It's beyond me."

"Maybe they know the bar manager."

"Well, whoever made the decision had to be hearing impaired."

She laughs again, gets up, and then drops the tofu dog in a nearby bin. As she walks back to me, I can't help but notice how lean and fit she is—it's obvious she takes care of herself. Suddenly, I feel like a sloth. I'm fit, but naturally, and not by the standards of today. I don't work out except on stage. As far as playing sports goes, since I graduated school, my only focus has been playing guitar.

She sits next to me just as I notice Rage and his two idiotic sidekicks leaving the bar. *Please do not see me. Please don't come over here.*

Tess follows my line of vision. "Is that the band?"

I nod. "Yep. Aren't they special?"

"Do you have something against goth groups?"

"Nope. Just them."

Thankfully, they don't notice me and head in the opposite direction.

Tess nudges me, then extends a hand. "It was nice to meet you, Lancelot. Thanks for the tofu dog."

I shake her hand. "No worries. I'm glad I could help you scratch off another item on your list of things to try."

"Give me your phone for a sec."

A bit taken aback, I reach into my pocket and slide out my cell. After I hand it to Tess, she punches in a number.

"I never do this, but I liked talking to you. Something tells me you'd be fun to hang out with."

I grin. "I am. I'm a blast."

"All right then. Stay in touch."

As soon as she rounds the corner, I take my first deep breath since I first laid eyes on her. I can't believe what just happened. I mean, I've had my share of women—most of whom approached me at a gig—but none as perfect as this creature. She's intelligent, funny, and possibly the most beautiful woman I have ever spoken to. Reg is never going to believe this.

On the ride home, I relive the surreal experience over and over in my mind.

However, once I enter the grim confines of the empty house, my focus quickly switches back to USH.

Sitting at the table, at the same spot I always sat to eat while growing up, I think about how void of joy and laughter the house is now. Then I grab a pen and paper and write the names of the band members. After I jot down Jet's name, I put an X through it and scribble the word *"exterminated"* beside it. I circle each name and write *"insulin?"* beside Rage. *One down and three to go.*

My cell rings. I look at the screen and see that it's Reg. He asks what I've been up to. I tell him about the stunning girl, Tess, and the wiener story. I omit the part about playing with Vancouver's shittiest band.

Reg is all pumped up when he tells me about an online masterclass he's taking with Byron Fry, a respected L.A. music producer and studio musician who's worked with numerous Grammy-winning artists. "You've got to check him out, man. He's brilliant. The guy was a road warrior for years, travelling all over the world with orchestras and bands. He teaches everything. Arranging. Producing. Everything."

I tell Reg that I'll look him up, even though there's no way I can fit one more thing in my head right now. We chat for a while longer, and then Reg suggests getting together tomorrow night. "Scot Little Bihlman is performing at Soul Bar downtown. Are you into going?"

"Sure. I should call the realtor lady in the morning and get things rolling. After that, I'm wide open."

When we finish talking, I end the call, then scroll immediately through my contacts to find Tess's number. I want to call her, but considering I just met her tonight, I don't want her to think I'm stalker material, so I go to bed with Tess on my mind.

I still can't believe that she randomly approached me. Girls that perfect have the pick of anyone they want, so why would she choose me?

My mind spins with questions. Maybe she's crazy and is just good at hiding it. Or perhaps she hooks up with random guys and drains their bank accounts. That wouldn't take long with me, considering I'm getting to the bottom of my savings.

Worse, what if she has a dick? I highly doubt it. Tess was all woman, and there was no mistaking that. Though, I remember when one of my buddies vacationed in the Philippines and met this knock-out chick at a bar. He was sixty bucks in on his booze tab—which is a lot, considering how cheap drinks are there—and this siren of a girl was drinking, dancing, and getting all intimate. He figured he'd take her to his room and finish the night with a bang. All was going to plan until the beauty came out of the john wearing a bra, her stiletto shoes, and nothing else. My friend was all excited until he looked down and saw that she was a he, and worse, that *he* part was bringing a lot more to the table than my friend. With that thought, I know if I do work up the guts to get in touch with her, I'd best proceed with caution.

As tired as I am after my surreal night, falling asleep takes long time. My mind bounces all over. When Hannah's face flashes through, I imagine her in the future she had gotten robbed from. Still beautiful, still innocent, only more grown up. Beside her is a clean-cut man her age, and in front of them is a pram with a newborn baby resting inside.

I smile momentarily before a dark cloud sweeps through and destroys the picture. Immediately, my guts clench and my pulse speeds up as another image pops into my head. USH. The three of them are laughing.

I will get each and every one of you low-life rats. You will regret what you did to my sister.

Chapter 7

A loud crack against my bedroom window shakes me from sleep. I quickly get up to investigate. When I see the blood smear on the window, I know immediately what had happened. A bird flew into the glass.

I pull on a pair of sweats before running down the stairs and out the front door. When I step onto the overgrown lawn, I see the creature lying in a patch of grass under my bedroom window. It's a falcon—a young, perfect specimen of its kind. My heart sinks as I walk over, reach down, and pick up the limp body.

Someone across the lawn clears their throat. "You shouldn't handle those things. They carry fleas and parasites." The cranky codger next door is watering his plants. Of all the neighbours we could've had, we get Oscar the Grouch. Dad used to refer to him as "Mr. Sunshine."

Without acknowledging the old man, I carefully cradle the bird in my hands and walk back inside the house. It doesn't take long to find an empty shoebox. After placing the bird carefully inside, I head to our small backyard with the box in hand.

The soil around our smaller trees is soft and loose. I set the box down and dig a pit sized to fit the box.

Once I finish with the mini-burial, I stand back and stare at the fresh mound of dirt. I feel terrible for the young bird just starting its life. I sigh. "Fuck, I'm sick of being surrounded by all this loss."

As I dust off my feet and step into the kitchen, my phone beeps. I look at the screen, expecting to see Reg's name. Instead, it's a message from Tess.

There must be some weird glitch or something. She gave me her number, but I didn't give her mine. I open the text. It's a smiley face. Confused, I text back a question mark, in case a spammer has somehow hooked onto her number.

I wait for a response, but nothing comes. Just as I put the phone down to get a drink, my phone rings.

I pick it up and see Tess's name. I answer, "Hello?"

"Hi. Remember me?"

Baffled, I ask her how she got my number.

"When I punched my number into your phone, I texted myself." She laughs. "Why? Does that freak you out?"

"Not at all, sneaky girl."

"What are you doing?"

I don't want to mention the bird—it's too negative—so I lie. "Just some yard work."

"That's cool. Well, I thought, maybe, I would return the favour and treat you to something to eat. I don't work too late tomorrow night, if you aren't busy—"

Before she finishes speaking, I answer, "That would be great. Do you want to meet somewhere, or should I pick you up at your place?"

"No. Not at my place. I mean, it's easy enough for me to meet you somewhere downtown."

"Okay. No problem. Do you have a place in mind?"

"What about that new seafood joint on Cardero Street?"

"Cool. I'm in."

She tells me she'll be there after work at 8 PM tomorrow. I agree, and we talk for a few minutes before hanging up.

I almost feel like a teenager on my first date. My gut is full of butterflies and nerves. I spend the rest of the morning packing up Mom's room and stacking the boxes in the garage. I quickly call the realtor and arrange to have her come by next week. Then Reg calls after lunch and arranges to pick me up for the Bihlman show a little later. For the first time since I've been back from Europe, I feel almost happy.

Reg pulls up at 6:30 PM, and we head to The Rainbow Centre on the West Side.

En route, Reg asks me what I've been up to today. When I mention the random call I got from Tess, he looks at me to make sure I'm not joking. "Are you serious? She just called out of the blue, and you didn't even give her your number? That's Fatal Attraction shit, don't you think?"

I chuckle. "I highly doubt a woman like her would be that into someone like me."

"Oh, come on. Don't say that about yourself. You know you're hot. Every time I'm with you, I get all flushed and—"

"Fuck off, Reg."

We get to the venue, and after seeing the sea of cars in the parking lot, Reg drives up to the university, and we park alongside the campus. As we walk back down the hill, Reg brings up an incident that happened in the area a few years ago. "Wasn't there a guy running around the university campus who was flashing people?"

I nod. "Yeah, I was amazed you never got caught."

"I'm a stealth runner. what can I say?"

We laugh. Nobody else would get the sarcasm we share. I guess that's why we kept our circles small while growing up.

The Rainbow Centre is one of the nicest venues for music in all of BC. The high-arched, baffled ceiling and the wooden walls add warmth to whatever music is played. Red cushioned seats and soft lighting make the large room intimate and welcoming.

By the time we find our chairs, the intro starts. The packed room breaks out in applause as Scot Little Bihlman walks out on stage with a guitar. I've watched a lot of his videos online and was always blown away by his versatility as a musician. He's a multi-instrumentalist who aces whatever he plays.

As he sits on the stool in the centre of the stage, Reg elbows me. "Did you know that he played with John Fogerty, Jellyroll, Dug Pinnick, and—"

I nudge him back. "Hey, Reg?"

"What?"

"Would you shut up so we can hear him? You can give me his full bio after the show."

Reg whispers, "Two-time Emmy winner..."

I stare at him, then shake my head. "Behave yourself. If you stay quiet, I'll take you out for an ice cream after the show."

"Oh really? Gee, Dad, an ice cream, just for me?"

"Yes, you can lick it off my ass."

Reg raises his voice. "You want me to lick ice cream off your ass?"

I silence him, and at the same time, the lady next to me shushes us both. Reg and I look at each other and snicker.

Bihlman starts the night with "Tooth and Nail," a wicked combo of rock and blues.

The crowd knows most of his songs—everyone is claps and sings along. By the time the show finishes, I feel inspired and guilty. I've got to spend more time playing my guitar.

We buy some merch on the way out. By the reaction of the fans and how pumped Reg and I are after the concert, Bihlman lives up to his reputation as a master of his craft. I'll be adding him to my rotation of music.

As we walk up the hill, I think about how many bands and shows Reg and I have been to together. How every one of the artists we follow and watch isn't only an incredible musician, but they're in it for the right reasons. It makes me sick to think of those stage posers, USH, who do twisted shit that damage the reputation of everyone in the industry.

We grab gut bombs at a drive-thru burger joint, and then Reg drops me off. It's weird, but regardless of how good a day I had, the darkness of revenge returns as I walk into the house and shut the door behind me. My thoughts immediately shift back to Hannah, and how I must finish what I had started.

* * *

The morning sun blasts through my bloodstained window, hurting my eyes. I didn't sleep worth a shit last night. I kept mulling over USH and how to pick them off one by one without getting caught. I roll over, put my pillow over my head, and sleep until the early afternoon.

After I've had my first coffee, I check my phone for any messages from Tess. So far, she hasn't written to cancel our plans for tonight.

I grab my guitar, go out to the back deck, and play for the next few hours before it's time to meet Tess downtown.

* * *

After I hit Marine Drive on the bike, a flash downpour strikes, soaking my jeans and thin, long-sleeved cotton shirt. When I arrive at the food joint, my clothes are stuck to me like cling wrap. I feel like a male stripper...without the buff body and killer looks.

Tess is breathtaking as she stands in the foyer, wearing a form-fitted red dress and matching stilettos. Her raven hair cascades over her shoulders and halfway down her back. I glance down at my outfit and, for a moment, consider backing away from the door before she sees me, but I know if I do, I'll be kicking myself in the ass forever.

When I walk up behind her, she turns and looks me in the eyes, giving me that same breathless feeling as when we first met.

She smiles. "You're all wet."

"Yeah, it's true. You know what they say about Vancouver—we don't tan here, we rust."

Thankfully, it doesn't take long before we're seated, and I can at least hide my sopping wet jeans. Tess orders a bottle of red wine, then jokes, "Did *you* want anything to drink?"

"No. No. You go ahead. I love going on dates where the girl gets smashed and embarrasses me."

Tess's laugh is like music. It seeps into my ears and touches my soul.

After we order a combo plate of the fresh catch of the day, we talk about our lives or what we want to reveal about them and then laugh and joke with each other. Tess has to be the easiest girl to talk to that I've ever met, and even though she's 100% woman, there's an edge to her that lends to the vibe of being one of the guys. From what I've seen so far, she's perfect, raising that burning question again—what the hell is she doing with me?

We keep talking long after we finish our meal. The waitress keeps returning to our table, undoubtedly wanting it freed for new guests. As promised, Tess grabs the check with the full intention of buying me dinner. It takes a bit of quick-handedness as I snatch the bill out of her hands.

Thankfully, when we walk outside, the rain has stopped, leaving the smell of fresh, clean air behind.

I glance at her. "So, can I call you a cab or something? I'd give you a lift on my bike, but I only have one helmet with me."

She thinks for a moment, then asks, "Have you finished with me already?"

I laugh. "No. Why? Do you have something else in mind?"

She nods. "I was going to watch a band. If you want to come, that would be great. Unless, of course, you have other plans?" She winks.

"Who are we going to see?"

"It's a surprise." She waves to one of three cabs idling nearby.

I love she's into music. That's a huge bonus. Even though I've been going to concerts and shows with Reg a lot lately, I don't mind seeing another show. I could never get sick of it. I hope that whoever we're going to watch isn't lame. People's tastes vary greatly, especially between musicians and non-musicians.

Considering the traffic of people coming and going on the well-lit Cardero Street, I'm not too concerned about leaving the bike. Once we're in the cab, Tess tells the driver to take us to Triggers Bar on Howe Street.

When we arrive, I'm blown away when I see Darby Mills on the marquee—*good choice, Tess!* Darby always gives a great show.

I nudge her and smile. "This should be cool."

Inside, we grab a couple of drinks, then make our way toward the stage. The room is packed as I lead us to an open space on the floor. Unfortunately, canned techno music is booming through the club, making it hard for Tess and me to hear one another.

After a few minutes, Tess waves me close, then speaks loudly in my ear. "I'll be right back." She passes me her drink, then heads toward the bathrooms.

All eyes are on her as she weaves through the mostly male crowd. A few moments later, the house lights dim, the stage lights come on and out walks the Scream Queen herself, Darby Mills.

The crowd bounces and cheers as they chant her name. Darby is a national icon who, through the years, has continued to produce killer tunes that rock the hell out of every venue she plays. It's hard to believe she started in the music industry at such a young age and is still going strong. I browsed through YouTube the other day and saw a couple of new videos by Darby Mills Project; I was blown away by "Trick of the Light." An old-school cool tune with a contemporary feel and a great addition to my playlist.

When Tess returns, I hand her the drink, and she flashes me a smile. About two songs in, the crowd bangs into us, and Tess grabs tightly onto my arm to steady herself—an ego-boosting moment for me.

After the show, Tess and I do our best to find a cab. We're successful after twenty minutes when a party of four pulls up. Once they've unloaded, we quickly slide into the back seat. "Where to first?" I ask. "Your place?"

"No, we'll drop you off at your bike first. I need to make a stop before calling it a night."

As we return to Cardero Street, where the bike is parked, Tess asks me why I left Canada to play music in another country.

"I loved recording in Europe. I wish the industry here in Canada had more to offer. I would've stayed and worked my way up the ranks. Unfortunately, the music scene here has gone to shit. Even the rock fests are dwindling. And, what I've heard from fellow musicians, if you are lucky enough to secure a spot, you have to worry about getting paid."

"Well, that's depressing."

"It is what it is. In the 80s, the country was hopping, with great venues and an endless supply of talent to play in them. Now, it's a whole different ballgame."

"Do you think the pendulum will swing back the other way, and the industry will thrive here again?"

I shrug. "I don't think it'll ever be the same as it was, but I'm hopeful the demand for live bands will make a comeback one day."

"So, until then, you'll be playing overseas?"

"It only makes sense. You've got to go where the work is. Though, I've got no plans to go anywhere right now. I have things I need to settle here first."

"Sounds interesting. What kind of things?"

Thankfully, at that moment, we reach Cardero Street, and I don't have to come up with a half-assed answer to Tess's question. We both leave the cab, and Tess tells the driver to wait. She walks me over to the bike, then kisses me on the cheek. "I had a nice time tonight."

I smile and give her a quick hug. "It was cool hanging out with you. Maybe we could do it again soon."

"I'd love to. Just call me."

I watch as she walks to the cab and slides gracefully into the back seat. I put on the helmet and then sit on the bike, watching the cab pull away. She returns my gaze through the window until the car turns a corner and disappears.

Driving down Georgia Street toward the Lionsgate Bridge, I try to burn Tess's face into my memory. I don't want to forget a single detail before seeing her again.

Once home, I change out of my damp jeans and into a pair of sweats, then check my phone for messages. Reg called and texted a thumbs up at some point during the evening. Then I see a text message from Rage.

"You forgot a cable and a necklace after the gig. Shoot me a message when you're

free to swing by. I've got a couple bucks for you as well."

I'm not surprised I forgot stuff there. I couldn't get out of that bar fast enough.

* * *

As I sit in the living room, staring into the fireplace, the cold vibes of the house creep into my pores. I can feel the threat of darkness lurking.

To ward off the impending depression, I pick up my laptop to listen to music—the only thing that can pull me out of a funk. On YouTube, I type Soren Andersen, the world-famous guitarist on tour with Glenn Hughes. While I listen to his album, *Constant Replay,* I shake my head in disbelief. The guy has a distinctive colourful style, unlike anyone else I've heard. What I like most about his playing is he continuously surprises me with innovative riffs and mind-blowing techniques. It's not surprising he is a highly sought-after producer and session player.

The music helps, but the cold still lurks on the edge of my consciousness, so I decide to sleep. On my way to bed, I glance into Mom's empty room. As a child, I spent so much time lying on her bed while she read me stories. I guess she would always be here, healthy and happy and being the perfect mother. I took so much for granted back then. I close the door and then continue to my room.

Chapter 8

Tess calls at 10 AM as I'm getting ready to mow the lawn. She sounds upset. I hurry back inside the house so I can hear her more clearly. "What's wrong?"

"I don't know. Maybe I shouldn't have called you. I mean, we just met, but I feel like I can talk to you. Plus, there's no one in my life I can really confide in right now."

I must admit that I find it odd she's calling with her problems after knowing me for such a short time. And as far as her having no one else to confide in, that's a hard sell. She's stunningly beautiful and has a kick-ass personality. I'm sure she has friends.

"That's okay. I'm here if you need to get something off your chest."

She sniffs a few times, then takes a deep breath. "I live with my parents. It's a bit embarrassing, but it's true. Rents are crazy high in the Lower Mainland, and I can't afford to rent my own apartment, so I live in my parents' basement."

"There's no need to defend yourself. I get it. If I didn't have my mother's house to live in right now, I'd have to move out of town to afford a place."

"Thanks for saying that, Lance." She sniffs hard. "Anyways, I feel foolish even saying this at my age, but my father is abusive when he drinks, and he's been drinking a lot lately. My mom went to my aunt's in Burnaby, and I've been the only person at home to take my dad's crap."

"Geez, that's bad. Why didn't you go to your aunt's place with your mom?"

"I have to work. Burnaby is way too far to commute every day when you don't have a car. It would take hours on the bus to go there and back."

"I'm sorry you're going through this, Tess. Is there anything else you can do? No other options?"

"Not that I can think of. Last night, after you left the restaurant and I took the cab, I stopped at a friend's place. I asked them if I could crash there for a few nights until my dad finished his binge. But they didn't have a free bed for me."

For a moment, I think about loaning her enough money so she can stay at a hotel, but I remind myself that I don't have a lot to give right now. "Is there anything I can do to help?"

"I guess I just need a friend right now. I'm not working today. Do you want to hang out?"

"Yeah. We can do that. Do you want me to come to you?"

"No. I'll make my way to the North Shore. I'll call you when I get there in about an hour."

When the call ends, I quickly dial Reg.

"Hey, Lance. What's up?"

I tell him about Tess, how she's out of a place to stay and can't go home. Then I ask if he can loan me another helmet in case I have to take her somewhere. He tells me to meet him at his place in fifteen minutes.

* * *

Reg stands in front of his perfectly manicured lawn, colourful flowers on each side of the house entrance. I get off the bike and walk up the driveway. "Hey, Martha Stewart, nice yard. Did you do all this yourself?"

Reg sighs. "Yeah, I was just gonna whip up a Bundt cake and a pot of tea."

We laugh. He walks me to the garage, grabs a helmet off the shelf, and passes it to me. "You know, as hot as you say this girl is when you told me how she approached you so easily downtown—and now, calling you about being stranded—I'm hearing alarm bells like crazy."

"Well, it's probably just tinnitus. There's nothing to worry about. She's a nice girl. You're paranoid because you don't know women."

"I know women. I had a date the other night."

"Mary and the four palm sisters don't count."

He laughs. "You're an asshole. Just tell me you won't let this girl stay with you. I've got a gut feeling on this."

"Yeah, yeah. Don't worry about it. I'm just going to talk to her. I'm not even meeting her at my place. She needs a friend right now."

"All right, man. But keep your guard up."

"I will, Mommy."

After strapping the spare helmet to the bike, I'm just about to get on when my phone beeps with a message from Tess. She's waiting for me at the park beside the Lonsdale Quay.

* * *

There's no beauty comparable to the Pacific Northwest. As I drive down the steep hill, I gaze at the sparkling ocean, where cruise ships and sailboats pass by. Stopping at a red light, I breathe in the clean sea air.

I'm a bit nervous about meeting Tess. Her exceptional beauty, along with her dynamic energy, makes me feel vulnerable. And even though I didn't admit it to Reg, I was thinking the same thing as him. I barely know this girl, and it does seem strange she's calling me while in a crisis, someone she barely knows.

As I pull up to the entrance to the park, I see the dark-haired beauty. She's wearing a cut-off and slim-fitting jeans.

She flashes me a smile. "Hey, handsome. It's nice to see you."

Considering how upset she was on the phone earlier, I had expected to see red eyes and a look of despair. Instead, she's glowing with enthusiasm.

I park the bike, then walk with her to the Seawall to find a place to sit. Tess spots a bench overlooking the water, and after a near-miss collision with a guy on a bicycle, we walk over and take a seat.

As we look out at the sea, Tess tells me about her father and how volatile their household has been lately. "He hasn't always been a lush. But after retiring a year ago, he's gone downhill fast."

"Is he violent toward you or your mom?"

She shakes her head. "He throws stuff at the wall sometimes but never at us. But it's the emotional abuse more than anything. After he hits the booze, he gets belligerent and hurls insults at whoever is in the room."

"That's awful." I put my hand on her shoulder.

"I hate conflict. It's why I've never been in a fight. What about you?"

"What about me?"

"Conflict. Do you avoid it or embrace it?"

"I avoid it most of the time, except when it's unavoidable."

"What would make it unavoidable? I mean...can't you just walk away?"

"No. Not always."

"Give me an example of a situation where you got confronted and couldn't walk away."

I think for a few moments before answering. "There's this stigma about musicians. The average person believes that we artists can't defend ourselves. So, we often get confronted by steroid monkeys, drunk shit disturbers, or jealous husbands with wives who pay us attention on stage."

"That's crazy. Has that ever happened to you? Did someone confront you?"

I laugh. "Of course. I play in a bar where they serve booze. Everyone becomes an asshole at some point."

"Tell me about a time that happened."

I'm not sure why she's digging so deeply, but I humour her. "Okay. One time I was playing at this hole-in-the-wall bar in the Fraser Valley. We'd just finished our last set and were tearing down when this drunk asshole in the crowd got up on stage and sat on the drum kit. He was a big guy, a thug. Anyways, we asked him nicely to leave, and he started calling us girly boys and pansies. I walked up to the guy and tried to reason with him. He pushed me, and I tripped on the floor cords and landed on my ass. I got up and tried to reason with him again, but all he wanted to do was fight. The guy was double my size and feeling no pain, so definitely fighting wasn't something I wanted to do. I asked him to leave, and he said, 'What are you going to do if I don't, pansy boy? Are you going to scratch me and pull my hair?'"

"Wow. So, what did you do?"

"The only thing I could. I broke his nose."

Tess stares at me, then grins. Just then, a lady walks by, pushing a small child in a stroller. Tess waves at the infant. She's sweet, and there's a naivety about her that I find endearing.

We talk for an hour or two until dark clouds roll in.

"Do you have a place to stay tonight? Should I drop you somewhere?"

She shakes her head with a sigh. "I've tried every person I know. No one has room for me. I guess my only option is to go back home."

The words escape my mouth before I have time to think about them. "I have room at my house if you're really stuck."

She looks at me, smiling wide with gratitude. "I was hoping you'd say that."

When the first raindrops hit, I tell her we should get going. As we walk back to the bike, I feel conflicted. I have no idea who this girl is. She could be a total whack job. But on the other hand, I can't let her go back home to be a verbal punching bag for her father.

*　*　*

As we pull up to the house, the sky opens. We quickly run inside, half-drenched and laughing.

After removing our sopping wet shoes, I get her a towel from upstairs. It's strange; even though she's only gotten here, the energy in the house feels different, in a good way.

I tell Tess to follow me as I give her the grand, boring tour. I show her Hannah's room and my mother's, which is now bare except for the bed. Then we walk past my room, where my bed is unmade, and clothes are strewn everywhere. She looks at me, eyebrows raised. "Maid's day off?"

I chuckle. I'm just about to head back downstairs when Tess grabs my wrist and pulls me toward her. She looks briefly into my eyes and then pushes her soft lips against mine.

It takes me a moment to believe what's actually happening. Then I put my hands around her waist and kiss her back. She tastes sweet, like honey. Her moist tongue and soft breath are like a drug. The longer we kiss, the more I want her.

I run my hands down to the small of her back and feel her velvet skin beneath my fingers. She slowly moves her hips, then presses her pelvis against me. As I slide my hands down to her young, taut ass, she moans and rubs her chest against mine. I want her so badly I can barely contain myself, evident by how stiff I'm getting.

We're locked in a hot and sweaty embrace. Before I know it, we're on my unmade bed and pulling off our clothes. On my back and standing at full attention, I look at Tess. Every inch of her hard, curvy body is perfect. Slowly and seductively, she crawls over me. The moment she kisses me again, I'm gone, wholly consumed in heat.

Her body moves like water. She's agile and responds to everything I do and every place I touch her. We devour every part of each other and get lost in back-arching orgasms with an insatiable hunger for more. When we finally come up for air and I get us a drink, I glance at the time on the way back to the room, 5 PM. We'd gotten lost in primal lust for hours.

I'm climbing back into bed when there's a hard banging at the front door. Tess sits up, looking alarmed. "Wow. Someone must want to speak to you pretty badly."

The knock comes again, and to prevent Tess from getting more freaked out, I get back up to check the door, dipping into the bathroom on the way and snatching a hand towel from the bar on the wall.

When the knock sounds a third time, I feel aggravated. *Who the hell is banging the shit out of the door?*

Then, a thought occurs to me. What if it's the cops?

What if they've somehow linked me to Jet's death?

I walk a little more cautiously down the stairs to the front door. With my pulse racing, I unfold the small hand towel and do my best to cover my privates before grabbing the handle and slowly opening the door.

When I see Reg, I'm both relieved and pissed off. "What the hell, man. Why were you knocking so loud?"

"Because I've been standing out here for ten minutes. I thought maybe you were in the garage and couldn't hear me." His eyes fall to the hand towel. "Dude, where are your clothes?"

I ignore his question. "What are you doing here?"

"I was in the area and thought I'd stop by to see if you wanted to grab a bite somewhere. But after seeing you half-naked, I'm not sure I'm hungry anymore."

"You're hilarious. Just go, and I'll call you later."

Reg glances over my shoulder, then gives me a sly grin. "Is someone here?"

"Don't worry about it."

"It's that girl you went to meet, isn't it?"

"No, Reg. It's the rickety old lady from next door."

"Then why are you whispering? She probably can't hear us anyway."

"Reg. Just go, and I'll reach out when..." I stop talking when Reg shifts his eyes, now transfixed on something behind me.

He grins. "Hi."

I turn around and see Tess standing there. She's wearing my Toto shirt and nothing else. "Is everything okay?"

"Yes. Everything is fine. This is my soon-to-be-ex-friend, Reggie. He was just leaving."

Reg says hello again. I can tell he's stupefied by her beauty.

I up my volume. "Okay, Reg. I guess I'll talk to you later."

Tess waves a hand. "Don't leave on my account."

"He's not. He has to be somewhere."

Reg shrugs. "Actually, it's not urgent that I go. I can probably stay for a few minutes."

My eyes widen, and I mouth *no*.

Tess nudges me. "Great! I'll go and put some clothes on." She turns and disappears up the stairs.

I turn back to Reg. "Dude, I swear, you are such an asshole. I'm going to get you back so bad."

Ignoring my threat, he turns to me with wide eyes. "She is amazing. Holy shit. You weren't kidding."

I smile. "You have no idea how perfect this woman is."

"I can't believe she's here."

I drop my voice to a whisper. "Me either."

"Forget what I said about being cautious. Fuck it! If she's a psycho or just wants your money, it's worth it."

Tess comes back in the same outfit she wore earlier. I gesture to the stairs. "I'll get dressed."

Reg steps inside and kicks off his shoes. "Please do. The longer I have to see you like this, the more therapy I'm going to need."

I punch him on the arm, then head up to my room.

* * *

By the time I'm dressed and back downstairs, Tess and Reg are deeply embroiled in a conversation about music.

I head for the couch. "Hey, are you guys hungry?"

Tess nods. "I just ordered a couple pizzas." When I sit down, Tess walks over and sits beside me, putting her hand on my leg.

It's hard to believe I'd only just met this woman. Not only have we already had wild sex, but she's also now chumming with my friend. Usually, I like my space, but I don't think I'll ever tire of having her around.

It's not long before the food shows up. The three of us eat, listen to music, and talk easily. Finally, Reg the Imposter gets up and says he has to go. He gives Tess an inappropriately long hug, which she laughs at, then he heads out.

When it's Tess and me again, she wraps her arms around my neck and kisses me. "Thanks for letting me stay over and hang out with you and your friend. He was nice."

"Anytime. Reg is the only person I hang out with here. He's a good guy, just a bit quirky."

We watch TV and snuggle on the couch together. It's bizarre, but even though I still feel a bit nervous and insecure around her, I feel like I've known Tess for a long time.

When I get up to put our dishes in the kitchen, Tess walks over to the mantel. She picks up a photo of my mom and dad on their wedding day, examines it carefully, and then looks at me. "You're a combination of both of them."

She puts it down, then turns her attention to Hannah's graduation picture. I walk up behind her. "That was my sister, Hannah."

"She was beautiful." Tess doesn't ask what happened to her. Maybe she senses my pain and thinks it would be unkind to make me talk about it. She gives me a grin. "We've both had a tiring afternoon, and I have to get up early for work. I think it's time for bed."

I follow her up the stairs to my room, where we both slip off our clothes and get under the covers. She slides over and puts her head on my chest, and I put my arm around her.

For the first time since coming home, I fall asleep as soon as I close my eyes.

Chapter 9

The early morning wind pushes tree branches against my window, causing an eerie screeching sound. I open my eyes and see a mass of jet-black hair strewn over my bare chest. I lie still so I don't wake her.

For half an hour, I gently run my fingers up and down the soft skin of her arm. I'm glad she's here. Even though my life is in chaos and I've been through hell, at this moment, I feel centred and normal.

When her phone alarm goes off, I gently shake her. With her eyes closed, she reaches over to the nightstand and shuts the alarm off. In a sweet, groggy voice, she tells me she needs a quick shower and will need to find a way to work. I quickly offer to drive her into the city on my bike. She kisses my cheek and thanks me, then gets up and heads to the bathroom without covering herself up.

I let out a long sigh. I don't want her to leave and forget about the incredible time we had shared. I want to know her more.

I prepare to get up and dress for the day when she walks out of the bathroom. Her wet hair sticks to her damp body.

She reminds me of a statue—a work of art.

I watch as she walks to the bedside, picks up her cell, then punches in a number. A few seconds later, she leaves a someone voicemail, telling them she's not feeling well and won't be coming in today. When she ends the call, she turns to me with a small smile. "Is it okay if I hang out here with you today?"

I reach over and pull her into bed with me. "No. I've had my way with you, so now I think it's best you leave."

She laughs and slides her naked body on top of mine. Soon, we immerse entirely in each other.

Sometime later, after sharing a steamy shower, we get dressed and have coffee. Tess mentions that she needs to make a quick trip to the mall for some makeup before she runs out of it. With nothing else on my plate, I happily agree to take her.

* * *

I wait patiently outside the cosmetic store as Tess walks around with a lady, picking out what she needs. I watch shoppers as they hustle past me and disappear into different stores.

Then, I spot a girl who looks vaguely familiar coming my way. It's not until she's about twenty feet away that I recognize her: Hannah's friend, Jenny.

It's not surprising that it took a moment to recognize her. She's the polar opposite of how she looked when I saw her at Lulu's. The multi-coloured hair is gone, replaced with a short brown bob. Her clothes are also different; instead of a short skirt and cropped shirt, she wears a form-fitted blouse and a pair of black slacks. She looks clean-cut and respectable.

I'm about to head toward her when Tess exits the makeup store. She follows my line of vision, and the moment she sees Jenny, she goes still. Confused, I look from her back to Jenny, who is, oddly, now veering down a side wing of the mall, walking quickly.

I return my attention to Tess. "That was weird. Do you know that girl?"

She takes a moment to answer. "No. Not at all. I did notice that she looked at me strangely, but I'm used to getting the cold shoulder from other girls. Why? Who is she?"

I'm still confused by Jenny's reaction. "A friend of my sisters."

As we head for the mall exit, we walk past a magazine shop, and I stop in my tracks. On a stand at the entrance is a newspaper, and on the cover is a big picture of Jet.

"Police appeal to the public for any information leading to the murder of Jet Wildly."

Tess looks at the paper. "That's awful. He looks young. I hope they catch the people who did it."

"A lot of these cases go unsolved. As for being young, youth has nothing to do with anything. Who knows? Maybe whoever took him out had a good reason."

Tess looks up at me with disbelief. "That's a strong opinion. Nobody deserves to die, no matter what they have or haven't done. If he was guilty of something, he could've been rehabilitated."

"Is that what you believe? That anyone can be rehabilitated?"

She nods. "Don't you?"

"Absolutely not. I mean, if this Jet guy was a thief, that's one thing. But for argument's sake, say he was a sexual predator or something. Do you still think he can get fixed?"

"Yes, I do. Don't you?"

"No. I don't. But then again, we don't know what this character Jet did, so it doesn't matter what we think."

As we continue toward the exit, I can feel the tension between us. She's not making eye contact with me anymore and not saying much. I try to think of something to pull her back in, but nothing comes to mind.

On the drive back to the house, when we stop at red lights or intersections, I try to spark a conversation, but after she forces out a word or two, the conversation goes flat.

Then, I spot a dollar store ahead. I quickly pull in and tell Tess that I'll be right back.

I browse through the party section and grab a can of silly string, a small air horn, and a bag of balloons. After I pay, I stuff the bag into my jacket so Tess can't see.

When we walk into the house, Tess goes to the living room and sits on the sofa. I go into the kitchen, deposit the bag on the counter, then grab a couple bottles of cold water and join her on the couch. "Are you okay, Tess? You seem a bit withdrawn."

"I'm just thinking about what you said back at the mall. About people deserving to be murdered."

I sigh. "I'm sure I sounded like a heartless bastard. I didn't mean to. It's just...I had someone very close to me die as a result of being brutally attacked. I guess I'm a bit biased on the subject."

She looks at me with sympathetic eyes. "Was it your sister?"

I nod. "How did you guess it was her?"

"When I looked at her picture before, you referred to her in the past tense."

"Yeah. Hannah was an angel. The perfect girl. Never got into trouble, and always kind and respectful to everyone."

Tess puts her hand on my leg. "And she was murdered?"

I take a deep breath. Then I tell her about that night. I tell her about Hannah, the free tickets she was given to a show, and the horrible events that followed. I don't tell her which band or that Jet was a member—thankfully, there was nothing about USH in the newspaper article. And I, of course, omit the part about me gutting Jet for his role in the crime.

"I understand why you have such strong opinions now." A tear rolls down her cheek. "I'm so sorry you lost her in such a terrible way." She puts her arms around me, and I can hear her sniffing as she presses her face into my chest. Then she sits back and wipes her eyes. "Did the band you mentioned get charged?"

I shake my head. "No. Hannah was too ashamed to go to the cops. She took drugs to numb the pain, which eventually took her."

"I've heard about a lot of girls who have gone to concerts and slept with the band—they're called groupies, aren't they?"

I nod. "Absolutely. Partying and sex have always been a by-product of the industry, and why not? If all parties involved are consenting adults, then so be it. But there's a big difference between groupies, free love, and the monsters who prey on young girls, drug them, and do horrible things against their will. Pigs like that shouldn't be in the music industry. As a matter of fact, they shouldn't be here at all."

"I understand where your rage is coming from, Lance, and it's warranted. But vigilante justice is wrong, I truly believe that. I think that everyone should have their day in court. And if random people with an ax to grind start taking matters into their own hands, we're in big trouble."

I kiss her on the forehead. "Let's change the subject, Tess. I want us to have a good, positive evening."

Even though we've agreed to disagree, I still feel awkwardness between us. So, while she's quietly watching a movie, I go to the kitchen and pull the lids off the silly string cans, then return to the living room for a full assault on my house guest.

Thankfully, Tess takes it well and retaliates. After a fierce, colourful foam fight, things get carried away. Before I know it, we're filling up the balloons with water and blasting them at one another in the backyard. I really like this girl. She's up for anything.

Exhausted and soaked, we take a hot shower together, then end up on my bed, having crazy sex until the wee hours of the morning.

* * *

I've been taking Tess to work and picking her up after her shift over the past week, fighting against strong winds and pelting rain. We've spent every evening together, holed up in the house, making love, ordering out, and talking about everything and anything. When I'm alone during the day, I tidy up the place and spend the rest of my time practicing guitar and writing songs.

Strangely, I haven't thought about USH that much. My passion for killing those rats hasn't entirely left me, but it's waned since Tess has been around. As nuts as it is to think it, for the first time, I may actually be falling in love, and I don't want anything to change that. Not to mention, if I do wipe out the other members of USH, there's always that chance I'll get caught, and it will be the end of Tess and me.

Tess and me. I like the sound of that.

* * *

I'm finishing this kick-ass guitar riff when I glance at the clock. I've got about an hour before I have to pick up Tess. Knowing she'll be hungry when she gets off, I decide to make a trip to the store now, so I'll have time to drop the groceries off beforehand.

Thankfully, there's a break in the weather. The rain slows down enough that I can see where I'm going on the bike. I drive to the main street and am ready to turn toward the grocery store when I see Jenny's Ford Pinto parked in front of the donut shop.

I merge into the centre lane, then turn into the parking lot. I park the bike beside her car and head into the donut shop.

Every table has multiple people sitting at them, except the small booth in the corner, where Jenny sits alone, reading a book.

I walk across the restaurant without her noticing. When I get to her table, I slide into the seat opposite her. She peers over the pages and recognizes me as she sets the book down. "Lance. What are you doing here?"

"I was riding by and saw your shit box car, so I thought I'd stop in and see how you're doing."

She laughs, then looks out the window at the bike. "Is that your ride?"

I shrug. "For now."

"Well, if I were you, I don't think I'd be talking shit about anyone else's wheels, that's for sure."

"Okay. You've got me there."

I ask what she's been up to lately. She tells me about being in NA and how she's going to counseling. I tell her about being at the hospital with my mom and how I thought that I'd seen her brought in on a stretcher.

She nods sheepishly. "Yeah, that was me. My mom told me that you called her. It was after I woke up in the hospital that last time that I decided to get my shit together. It hasn't been easy, but I've been making it okay so far."

"I'm really proud of you, Jenny. Remember, I'm always here if you need a friend." I look at her closely. "I saw you at the mall the other day. I know you saw me, but you changed your mind about saying hello. Why?"

She gives a half-shrug. "I wanted to say hi. Really, I did. It's just when I saw Tess I got confused and freaked out."

I stare at her, taken aback. "How do you know her name?"

"Who, Tess?"

"Yeah. Tess said she'd never seen you before."

Jenny raises an eyebrow. "Pfft. That's crazy. She went to university with me and Hannah. Granted, she was a couple years older than us, but I still hung out with her sometimes. She was more my friend than Hannah's. Tess liked to party, and your sister didn't."

My head spins as I try to make the dots connect. Tess got a good look at Jenny while we were at the mall. If she knew Jenny, why did she lie and say she didn't?

Jenny tilts her head, looking confused. "Is something bothering you?"

"No. Nothing." I focus on her again. "You said seeing Tess freaked you out. Why?"

Jenny sighs. "The last time I saw her, about a month ago, I was stoned and partying at a club in West Vancouver. I looked up and spotted her on the dance floor, so I went over and said hi. We went to the john together and started reminiscing. Eventually, Hannah's name came up, and she started talking about how bad she felt that Hannah died so young. I kind of...mentioned you at some point, too."

"Me? What do you mean you mentioned me?"

"It was just an offhand comment."

"But *why*?"

191

"Well, she said that she'd recently lost her sibling, so it just came up."

I shake my head. "I didn't even know Tess had a sibling, much less one who recently died. I told her about losing Hannah, so why didn't she mention it? This is all so confusing."

"But you did know."

I stare at her. "What are you talking about?"

"You knew Tess's brother. Or at least *of* him."

"Who is he, or *was* he?"

There's a small smile on her face. "His name was Jet."

It's like I got punched in the stomach. My head spins, and my hands tremble. "Jet? The guitar player from USH?"

Jenny nods. "Now you're getting it."

My stomach churns. I think about the newspaper headline. "If Jet was her brother, why the hell didn't she mention his name to me? And why the hell would *you* mention *my* name to her?"

"Because she was grieving for her brother, but all I could think about was what he and the rest of that band did to Hannah. I was stoned, drunk, and angry, and I blurted out what I saw the members of USH do to Hannah. She slapped me and spit in my face. Said that Jet would never have done anything so despicable to any girl. We argued for a while, and in the heat of the moment, I told her Hannah's brother was in town, and he was looking to get even."

I shake my head, trying to absorb what she's saying. "Maybe she doesn't even believe you saw USH. She probably assumes you saw a different band that night and got it mixed up."

She shakes her head. "No. She knows we saw USH. It was Tess who gave us the tickets in the first place. Remember? I told you about the girl whose brother was a guitar player and was performing downtown. She wanted to go but couldn't, so Hannah and I went."

I feel lightheaded and disoriented.

Jenny taps her fingers on the table. "The one thing I can't figure out is why you were even at the mall with Tess."

My mind flashes back to the gig I did with USH downtown, then to the hotdog stand. "I met her after playing with that shitty band."

"Ah. Clever move, Lance. You butcher the guitar player, then take his place. Once you're in, you can get close enough to pick the rest off, one by one." Jenny grins. "I like it. But you weren't expecting Jet's sister to magically appear, were you?"

I glare at her. "Are you sure you're not high? Because everything you're saying is Twilight Zone shit."

Jenny leans across the table, her eyes boring into mine. "Don't worry. I won't tell anyone. Hannah was my best friend. What happened that night set her on a fast path to destruction. Don't you think I'm grateful that you're getting rid of the slimy fucks responsible? I'm rooting for you, Lance. I'm just saying you may have walked right into a trap set by Tess. I knew she was smart but had no idea she could mastermind a plan like this."

"Plan? What plan could she have?"

"I don't know. But she has one, for sure. There's no other way she'd hang out with the guy she suspects killed her brother. She's got a plan. You can believe that."

I shake my head in disbelief. "I don't buy it. If she thinks I killed Jet, why didn't she go to the cops?"

"Why didn't you?"

I don't answer.

"Think about it, Lance. No evidence to you or your ass would already be busted. Also, her father is a high-ranking judge. A family like that avoids dirt at any cost. If you were arrested, your defence would reveal that Jet raped a young girl. That kind of thing stains a family name forever."

"But Tess told me her father is a lush. They live downtown someplace."

Jenny shakes her head, grinning. "Actually, they live in Caulfield Village, in a posh mansion with a big iron gate—rich snobby types."

"They live in a mansion, and Tess works at a coffee bar downtown?"

Jenny snorts. "Tess doesn't work for the coffee shop. She owns it. Or her dad does. I heard they've opened up a few more locations in the Lower Mainland." She shrugs. "You'd think she'd own a more astute business, but she and Jet rebelled from the more lavish lifestyle. Both wanted to dumb down, be like the rest of us commoners." She laughs.

I'm no longer listening. My mind drifts back to the night I played downtown with USH and met Tess at the hotdog stand. Right away, I sensed there was something strange about her approaching me. She was too beautiful, too persistent in wanting to talk to me, a strange man she met while alone downtown. I guess it all makes sense now.

Jenny seems to sense my despair. "Don't feel bad, Lance. But if you're smart, you'll get as far away from her as possible. There are millions of girls who'd love to be with you for the right reasons, but Tess isn't one of them. She has an agenda. And considering what you did to her brother, I don't think your safety is high on her list." Jenny gets up from the table and tucks her book under her arm. Then she leans down to whisper in my ear. "Just remember that line in William Congreve's play. 'Hell hath no fury like a woman scorned.' It's a good quote. Reminds me never to underestimate what women are capable of, especially when they're pissed off."

I sit for a few minutes after Jenny leaves, trying to come to terms with everything. One factor keeps pushing its way to the front of my mind—I greatly care about Tess. And if it's all been a game, a lie, then she was never truly with me. All of the talks we had, all the feelings we shared, all the wild sex and laughter...it's hard to believe that none of it was real, at least not on her part.

Feeling heavy, I check my phone for the time. Tess will need to be picked up soon, even though now I know she has her own wheels.

As I head down Lonsdale, I decide that when I see Tess, I'll act like everything is normal. I want to spend as much time with her as possible until the shit hits the fan. It starts to rain again as soon as I turn onto Marine Drive.

After maneuvering around branches and debris on the wet streets, I finally reach the coffee joint. Tess waits for me at the door, a knapsack thrown over one shoulder.

She jogs over to the bike, grinning. "You know, we really have to get you another form of transportation. Especially for days like today."

I love the feeling of her body against mine as she wraps her arms around me and slides in tight. We wait behind scores of cars going over the Lionsgate Bridge, then run into the same traffic fuckery on Marine Drive. By the time we reach the house, we're both muddy and wet from the spray off the road.

Once we're inside, Tess puts her bag in the bedroom, then meets me in the front room. With my arm around her, she tells me how her day went, then asks if I got much time to practice my guitar. I tell her about the songs I've been working on and offer to show her some of the riffs I've worked up.

She nods. "Of course. I want to hear you play. First, though, I want to talk to you about something."

A large ball forms in my throat, making it hard to swallow. *Please don't confront me now, Tess. I know what's going to happen if you clear the air. You'll leave, and I'll never see you again.*

She looks up at me with her beautiful eyes. "I don't know how you're going to react to what I have to say, but I have no choice. I have to take a risk and say it anyway. And I want you to be honest with me, no matter how much you think I won't like the answer, okay?"

I don't think she wants my complete truth about what Jet did to Hannah and what I did to him. But I lie and agree to get the pain over with quicker.

She appears uncomfortable, shifting her eyes from mine and fiddling with her hands. "Okay. Here it goes. I want to know if it would be all right with you if I moved in here."

I'm taken aback, and my mouth involuntarily drops open. I do my best to compose myself. "Move in here with me?"

"It's way too soon. I can tell by the look on your face that I'm rushing things. I shouldn't have said—"

"Tess."

She looks up at me. "Yes?"

"I think that would be great." I smile, then let out a long sigh of relief.

She mirrors my relief. "I'm so glad you feel this way. For a moment there, I didn't know how you would react."

We kiss deeply for a long while. Then she pulls back with a grin. "I've got some great news. I don't have to work for the next couple of days. I'll be here with you."

Of course, you don't have to work. You own the shop.

After eating some take-out, we go to bed and watch a movie, then make love until the wee hours of the morning. Just before I doze off with her in my arms, I think about how content I am right now and how I would give almost anything for this moment not to change. I pray Jenny is wrong about Tess having an ulterior motive for being here with me.

Chapter 10

I wake up to the sound of clanking pots coming from the kitchen. I quickly wrap a towel around my waist and head downstairs.

When I turn the corner to the kitchen, I see Tess taking dishes out of the cupboards and stacking them on the counter. I clear my throat loudly, and she turns around. "Good morning, Lancelot. I've been cleaning out the cupboards. Do you know some of these dishes were put away dirty?"

Not surprising, considering my mother's recent history with booze. "Nope. I Didn't know that. I usually get take-out."

"Well, that's got to change. I'm going to make you such good food. It will blow your mind."

"You can cook?"

"No, but Jamie Oliver can. All I need to do is watch a few of his cooking shows on YouTube, and I'm pretty sure I can replicate his dishes."

I stare at her, wide-eyed. "I'm glad my healthcare is paid up."

She smiles, then shakes her head and asks me to grab the newspaper from the front step.

Still trying to wake up, I yawn and rub my eyes as I slowly saunter to the foyer. I turn the front door handle and am outside before realizing we don't get the paper.

I turn to walk back inside and see Tess standing there, grinning devilishly. She quickly snatches the towel around my waist, closes the door, and locks it.

The air is filled with the sounds of a warm day. Lawnmowers rumble in the distance, and I hear people talking and moving about in the cul-de-sac. Horrified at the idea of being spotted bare-naked on the stoop, I knock hard on the door. "Tess. You're hilarious. Now open the door."

I hear her cackling from inside the house. "Say the magic words, and I'll let you in."

I laugh nervously. "I don't know the magic words. Just let me in."

"That's too bad. Rack your brain, I'm sure they'll come to you."

I close my eyes, cup my junk, and squeeze in as close to the door as possible. "Tess. Seriously. There are people around. You've got to open the door."

"I'd like to, Lance, but unfortunately, the door will only unlock if you say the magic words."

"I don't know...Rumpelstiltskin? I have no idea. Just open up."

Suddenly, I hear the crunching sound of someone walking up behind me. I take a deep breath, then turn to see my cantankerous old neighbour glaring at me.

No way, man. Anyone but him.

The old codger and I lock eyes for what feels like an eternity.

"Nice ass," he says, then walks away.

I chuckle and shake my head before turning my attention back to the door. "Tess. Are you going to let me in, or do I have to scale the fence to the backyard?"

"I've seen that fence. It looks dangerous. Anything dangling could get caught. Are you sure you don't want to give the magic word another try?"

"This is ridiculous. Okay. Fine. I'll guess again, and then I'm going around the back."

She giggles. "I'm waiting."

I guess the first words that come to mind that she' d want to hear. "Tess, you're the most beautiful girl in the world and—"

"Close enough." The door opens.

I sprint inside and immediately seek her out. When I hear a high-pitched scream running up the stairs, I race to catch her. Opening my bedroom door, I see Tess lying on my bed naked, the t-shirt on the floor in front of her.

I laugh and shake my head. "Do you really think you can escape punishment just because you're lying naked in my bed? Are you trying to bribe me?"

She nods and smiles.

I shrug, then walk to her. "Do you think such naughty tactics will work on me?"

She sits up, grabs onto me, and pulls me down on the bed.

We spend the next hour having wild sex, thrashing around so energetically that the clock above my bed slides off the wall and crashes on the floor. Afterward, we lie quietly with our chests heaving, trying to catch our breath.

I slide my hand over and rest it on her toned stomach. "Wow. I performed well," I joke. "I'm really something."

"Is that right? Because I thought I was the one doing all the work." Tess sits up and looks at the clock on the floor. "We should probably hang that back on the wall, hey?"

"I can do it. Just relax."

She insists on helping, so I tell her, if she wants to do something, she can get the hammer out of the utility drawer in the kitchen. She leaves, and I get up and pull on a pair of shorts. I grab the clock, snap the faceplate onto the back, and then search for the nail between the bed and the wall. While I'm searching, I hear Tess come back into the room.

"Did you find the hammer?" I ask.

She doesn't answer.

Finally, I spot the nail and grab it, then turn triumphantly to face Tess.

Immediately, I can tell something is wrong. Her face is pale, and her eyes are huge and wild. In one hand is the hammer, and in the other, a piece of paper.

"What's wrong?"

She says nothing. Her chest heaves in and out as if she's hyperventilating.

"Tess. What is it."

"You sonofabitch." She holds up the piece of paper. "I almost convinced myself you were innocent, but you're not. You did it. You fucking did it!"

I slowly stand. "Did what? What is it I did?" My eyes catch a bit of the writing on the paper. It's the list I made of the names of USH's band members. In a flash, I recall what else is written on the page—Jet's name, with the word *"exterminated"* beside it.

"You killed Jet."

She's looking right through me. I know that if I lie, she'll see it. Besides, it was going to come up anyway. I guess it might as well happen now.

"Tess. I don't know what to say, except that I'm crazy about you. I know we've only just met, but I don't want this thing we have to end—"

"Are you fucking kidding me? What kind of a person would I be to stay in a relationship with someone who killed my brother?"

I put my hands up and take a step toward her. "Let me explain what happened."

"What happened is you butchered him. That's the bottom line. And no amount of talking is going to change that. You're a murderer."

I shake my head. "I hate that word. I prefer to be thought of as an exterminator."

"Are you crazy?" She's yelling now.

"Please just sit on the bed and talk to me for a minute."

"No. I don't want you anywhere near me." She sniffs and wipes her eyes. "When Jenny told me you were out for blood over what happened to Hannah, I was all set to hunt you down. To find out if you were the one who butchered my brother. But after spending so much time with you, I convinced myself there was no way you could commit such a heinous crime. I am such an idiot."

"So, you lured me in, thinking if I got close to you, I would open up and confess? What were you going to do once I admitted to killing Jet?"

She shakes her head. "I don't know. I don't know. I just needed to know the truth."

"Then what's the plan now? Are you calling the cops to have me arrested?" I gesture to the paper in her hand. "That piece of paper isn't solid evidence. Nowhere does it say that I killed anyone—just the names of USH with a line through Jet and some random words. It's hardly the proof the cops would need. I could've written this after learning about Jet's murder. Maybe I was a fan of the band, as hard as that is to imagine." I take another step closer. "I know your father is a big-time judge. Having me arrested wouldn't shine well on him once I mentioned how his son raped and drugged my baby sister."

"You don't know he did that for sure."

"Yes, Tess. I do. Jenny was there. She would never lie about what happened that night."

"I hate you."

"No, you don't, Tess. That's the problem. You feel just as strongly for me as I do for you. If you can somehow let the past die, we can still be together. We both lost people we loved. It's over for them, but that doesn't mean we must stop living. Since I've been with you, my perspective on seeking revenge has changed. I don't want to do anything that will jeopardize our relationship."

"Too late. I never want to see you again."

I cringe and close my eyes. *Please don't go, Tess. I'll be all alone again if you go.*

I open my eyes just in time to see the hammer swinging hard for my face. Unfortunately, I don't have enough time to move, and the heavy metal tool connects solidly with my cheekbone. Instantly, my eyes water, making it impossible to see, and I collapse onto the bed behind me, holding my face.

"Tess?" I holler. "Please don't leave." But all I hear is my laboured breathing.

Standing takes a minute, and I stumble to the bathroom to look in the mirror. There's a huge gash on my cheek under my right eye. Blood is streaming out, dripping on the counter and into the sink.

I quickly wet a towel and press it onto the wound, then head downstairs, hoping Tess may still be here.

Dark, familiar energy greets me as I enter the front room. There's no need to look for her further—she's gone. I can feel it.

I flop down in the La-Z-Boy. My face pulsates in pain, but it's nothing compared to the agony I feel about Tess leaving me.

My heart skips a beat when the phone rings, hoping it's Tess calling to talk. One hand still holds the towel to my cheek, and I snatch the phone with the other. "Hello?

"Dude. Where have you been? I've been texting for the past two days. Is everything cool?"

"No. I wouldn't define everything as being cool."

In true Reg form, he probes me for info. I give it because I'm too exhausted to develop a believable lie. Of course, I leave out Tess's motive for hurling the hammer at me.

"She cracked you in the face with a fucking hammer? Is she nuts?"

"At that moment, probably. But as a rule, no. Tress is the sanest girl I've ever met."

"But why would she even—"

"She had her reasons, Reg. I'm not getting into it."

"Stay there. I'm coming over."

"Don't bother. I don't want company right now. I just need to go back to my room and lie down."

Reg hangs up, completely ignoring what I've just told him. I unlock the front door, then head back upstairs to my room.

* * *

Reg knocks twice, then slowly pushes the bedroom door open. It hurts like hell when I turn my head to look at him.

"How ya feelin', Lance? I brought you some food. You should probably try and put something in your stomach. Might make you feel better."

I try to sit up, but as soon as my head leaves the pillow, throbbing pain overwhelms me.

Reg sits on the bed and puts the paper take-out bag beside me. "How bad is it?"

"Well, it kind of feels like I've been hit in the head with a hammer, but I guess that's expected, considering that's what happened to me."

"You don't look as bad as I thought you would, considering. A little swollen in the eye and cheek area. Makes your head look like an orange on a toothpick."

I manage a laugh.

"I think you'll be okay. You got lucky." He pauses. "Are you sure you won't consider pressing charges?"

I shake my head. "Nah. Like I said, she had her reasons. And even though I don't like the way she dealt with it, I don't blame her. Grief makes us do some fucked up shit. I'm living proof of that." I sigh. "I think what gets me the most is that I was really into her.

She was the first girl I could actually see myself with for life."

We don't say much for a few moments until Reg breaks the silence telling me how he ran into the McKern brothers—Kevin and Bruce—at the Ambleside Music Fest yesterday. "They told me they'd just been to New York and caught a TSO show. Said it was insanely good. The coolest part of the concert was when Joel Hoekstra and Chris Caffery were belted onto stands, then raised high on a huge hydraulic platform and played off each other, ripping it up as the crowd went wild."

"That sounds killer. There's nothing Hoekstra can't do. The guy's a legend. It doesn't matter if he's playing with Whitesnake, Cher, or TSO—he brings a unique sound and skill that transports everything to a higher level. I love the song 'Finish Line' from *Joel Hoekstra's 13*. You've got to check it out. It's greasy and mean."

Reg nods. "Caffery, too. It's not only TSO he's known for. I remember hearing him in Savatage and then later, Doctor Butcher. I kept thinking, who the hell is this guy? He's diverse and can shred like a mother fucker. He explodes on every track."

Reg and I smile, then, in unison, say, "Where's Wilbur?"

* * *

Angry clouds swirl overhead as memories of my time with Tess haunt me. I miss her. I miss her terribly.

I understand why she left and didn't come back. She couldn't. Even if she believed me about Jet raping Hannah, he was her brother; how could she stay with the person who took his life? I get it. I just don't like it.

I haven't picked up my guitar in days. I'm not feeling very inspired. I've been mulling over the idea of returning to Zurich, getting away from here and every horrible thing that's happened. At least in Europe, I'd be so immersed in session work I wouldn't have time to feel all the sadness built up inside me.

Plus, there's nothing here for me now. My family is gone, and so is Tess.

Chapter 11

After a long, restless sleep, my mind churning and twisting, I decide to call the engineer at the studio in Zurich. Thankfully, he wants me to come back, so we make a tentative plan for me to return by the end of the week.

I spend the rest of the day doing my laundry, separating the items I'll take from the ones I'm leaving behind. The swelling on my face has gone down over the past few days. The gash on my cheek looks more like a nasty scratch now.

Tomorrow, I'll call the realtor. I'll tell her to come over, and I'll sign the listing papers.

I'm surprised to see it's already midnight when I finish the laundry. I decide to order a pizza, since I haven't taken any time throughout the day to grab a bite.

As I'm punching in the numbers, a text comes in. It's Rage.

"If you don't come by now to get your shit, I'm tossing it in the garbage. Got something else you might like, too."

I had completely forgotten about having to pick the stuff up. If it was anything but Hannah's necklace. I wouldn't care. But there's no way I want to leave the country without it.

The last people I want to see right now are the little pukes from USH, but I guess it's the final shitty thing I have to face before leaving. At least I'm not hellbent on exterminating them anymore. Not after Tess left. The fury I felt before I met her has all but disappeared.

Karma will get them. In one way or another, they'll pay. Though I must admit, I'd like to be there to see it happen, especially to Rage. I hate that self-righteous control freak. I hope he gets it the worst.

I shake my head as I think of his rat-like face. *I can't believe he thinks I actually want to join his band. What a delusional idiot.*

Five minutes later, I'm out the door and riding up Lonsdale toward the band's house. As I near the decapitated USH shack, I dream of looking out the plane window and how good it will feel to put distance between these disgusting pigs and me.

When I arrive, Blacky opens the door, then turns and walks away. As I enter the house, a thick waft of what smells like stale piss and rotting garbage burns my throat, making it hard not to gag.

Soon after, crashing sounds come from up the dark, narrow hall. I turn when a door opens just off the living room. Raven walks out, damp and naked, except for a ragged towel around his waist. He glances at me. "Hey, man. Does Rage know you're here?"

I shake my head. "Not yet. He texted, telling me to come over right away. He told me I could pick up my guitar cable and a necklace I forgot at the gig. He also said he had something else for me."

Raven cackles and nods, then points toward an old, stained sofa. "Take a seat. I'll let him know you're here."

I look down at the couch. God only knows what kind of nasty organisms are breeding on that thing. I opt to stand.

Rage appears a few moments later, wearing an open black shirt and pants as tight as the skin on a wiener. "You got here just in time." He waves me over. "Come with me. I've got something to show you."

As I walk behind him down a hallway, I glance around. The walls have been spray-painted black, and the lino flooring under my feet is broken and filthy. *This place should be condemned.*

Rage reaches his bedroom door, and is just opening it when Blacky calls out from the front room. "I'm running up the street to grab some more booze. I'll be right back."

"Don't be gone long," Rage calls, then disappears into the room. Slowly, I follow.

When I step into the room, my focus goes immediately to the bed. I can't believe what I'm seeing.

A young girl, about seventeen, is lying on her back. Her t-shirt is pulled up, exposing her small breasts. Her hair is golden and wavy, like Hannah's. She even has the same porcelain skin.

At first, I'm completely frozen, unable to move or speak. All I can do is stare as Rage grabs her long, white skirt and slides it off her little body. The girl moans as he then takes her panties in hand and yanks hard until they rip off her.

I watch Rage unzip his pants and pull them down over his white, scrawny ass. Then he grabs the girl's legs and pulls her to the edge of the bed. I briefly squeeze my eyes shut, hoping this will all be a bad dream when I open them—a figment of my imagination.

But it's not. When I open my eyes, the girl remains exposed and vulnerable, with Rage lurking over her.

I picture my little sister in the girl's place. *Is this how it happened, Hannah? Is this how he hurt you?*

Rage turns to me and smiles. "She's yours next."

Suddenly, my body loosens, and I draw in a deep breath. "Get away from her."

Rage's smile disappears. A look of confusion replaces it. "What the hell, dude? I thought you'd be up for this."

I step toward him. "Move the fuck away from her, or I'll rip your throat out." My voice booms.

He slowly turns to me. "Okay. Okay. Calm down. If this isn't your bag, that's cool. There's no need to freak out."

The girl moans and turns toward me, straining to open her eyes.

"What the hell did you give her?"

Rage smirks. "What are you, the police?"

I lunge toward him, my hand flying up to his throat. With all my force, I slam him against a wall, pressing as hard as possible. His eyes grow big as he grasps my wrist, trying to free himself.

I put my face close to his. "You twisted fuck. I'm going to enjoy squeezing the life out of you."

Rage attempts to turn his head to loosen my grip, and I quickly add my other hand, locking onto him like a vise. His face is soon deep auburn as he struggles for air.

I grit my teeth and grin. "What's the matter, Rage? You don't like it when the tables are turned?" I squeeze tighter. "Before I take the girl out of here, I'm going to make sure you're incapable of hurting anyone ever again. Consider it payback for what you did to my sister. Her name will be the last thing you ever hear."

I feel his strength weaken within my grasp. *Die, you mutherfucker!*

My body is exploding with adrenaline, my heart thundering in my chest. As much as killing Rage here and now wasn't the plan, now that it's happening, I feel like Superman, all my resentment and hate fueling my strength. I want to feel the life drain out of him. I need to taste his death.

"Give it up. The battle is over. You've lost. You screwed up royally when you messed with my sister." I spit in his face and watch as it slides down his cheek. "I'm not your guitar player, and I'm definitely not your friend. Do you know who I am, Rage? I'm your fucking Karma."

His legs buckle. I'm about to let him drop so I can finish him off on the floor when an unsettling energy enters the room. I release my grip on Rage and am turning around when what feels like a Mack Truck hits the back of my head, the crack of bone and a high-pitched squelch filling my ears.

Instantly weakened by the blow, my knees fold. Like a slain warrior, my power disappears, and I fall defeated to the ground. My cheek rests on the stained shag carpet, my eyes unmoving as they stare at used condoms, old pizza boxes, and a broken wine glass littering the space under the bed.

At first, my ears are deaf to all other sounds in the room. Then, slowly, the squelching starts to dissipate, and gradually, I make out a voice.

"Rage, are you okay, man? What the hell did he do to you?" It's Raven, his voice high-pitched and anxious. "I took him out. I swung my club hard and cracked the fucker's skull. He's no threat now."

I feel a warm, steady stream of blood as it trickles off my earlobe and drips silently, disappearing into the carpet. I know I'm hurt badly. Not because of pain—I feel very little of that—but because of the strange hollow sensation in the back of my head.

I heard bone crack. There's no mistaking that sound. The last time I heard bones break was when I was drinking with friends and foolishly climbed an old water tower. The rusted ladder gave way halfway up, sending me hurling toward earth, a large stone breaking my fall and ankle in two places.

Rage coughs, sputters, and tries to speak, but the only noise that comes out is a hoarse crackling.

"Don't worry, man," Raven says. "You're going to be okay. And I'll take care of the sonofabitch."

I'm unsure what he means by "take care of." Does he know that I'm still alive? Or does he think he's killed me and plans on disposing of my body? Whatever it is, I will not lie here and find out.

A dull, burning pain starts at the base of my neck. Like a dark, heavy hand, it moves slowly up the back of my skull. It will be challenging enough to escape this, but with unbearable pain added to the equation, my chances of escape are even less.

As blood continues to roll down my head, Raven continues to coddle Rage. Images of the young girl lying on the bed above, exposed and vulnerable, flash through my mind. She will suffer terribly if I fail to find a way out of this.

I can't live with that. I've got to save the girl. I've got to fight with everything I have.

I move my fingers first, then my toes. Next, I focus on my legs, one by one. They're stiff but working. I'm far from feeling like Superman, as I did when I held Rage's life in my hands, but at least I have hope.

Rage lets out a few more coughs, then manages to eke out his first audible words. "Kill that fucker. Bash in his head."

"You want me to hit him again?" Raven sounds nervous. "But what about the cops? Right now, I can say that I walked in while he was choking you, so I hit him with the golf club to save you. If I knock his brains out now, they'll know it was premeditated. I just thought we could let him bleed to death, and if he goes to move, we'll tie him up. Without medical help, he won't last long—"

"Do as I say," Rage barks.

Raven lets out a sigh. "Fine. I hope you have a plan. I don't want to go to jail for this."

I hear Raven walk across the floor and pick up the club. There's no way I can fend him off once he starts hitting me. I've got to act now.

I focus again on the broken wine glass under the bed. Then I reach as far as I can until I feel the stem with my fingertips.

Slowly, I roll the glass toward me as Raven walks up and rests his foot on my back.

"Hey, Lance. I never asked you this before, but...do you like to play golf?"

Finally, I manage to grasp the thin stem. With everything I have, I turn over and bury the jagged glass deep into his calf.

Raven screams, grabs onto his leg, and flops down beside me. "You *bastard*. You cut the shit out of my leg."

I hear Rage move on the floor. "You idiot. Fuck it. I'll do it myself."

"It hurts, Rage. I think I'm cut really bad. I need to go to the hospital."

"Suck it up," he croaks. "No one's going to the hospital."

As Rage struggles to his feet, I turn my head to see where the golf club landed. No matter what, I've got to reach it before that demented asshole does. It's my only chance at making it out of here alive.

I roll back onto my stomach, then pull each knee toward my chest. Then, slowly so I don't pass out, I slide my arms forward and push myself off the floor. Using my legs, I maneuver to the edge of the bed and then move with all the strength of both my arms and legs. I make it to a standing position.

Rage scrambles for the club, crawling over his bleeding and sniveling friend. He's within reach of the weapon. When weak and shaky, I lunge toward him. My foot lands on his hand as he grasps the golf club handle.

He looks up at me, seething and spitting like a rabid dog. "Get off my hand, prick."

I grin, then reach down and yank the club out of his grasp. "I guess this isn't your day, Rage."

He quickly rolls onto his back and scurries like a crab into the corner. A feeling of power slowly rises in me again, pushing aside my injuries for the moment. Dragging the iron, I slowly walk toward him, grinning from the inside out. "Now, what did you say a minute ago? You wanted your little patsy to finish me?"

"No. No." He's stammering in his hoarse voice. "You heard wrong, Lance. I didn't say that."

"No? My mistake. I guess it's possible I misheard you with all the blood in my ears." I shrug, then pick up the club and twirl it. "But no matter. Since we're both here and have nothing else to do, maybe you could teach me a few things about golf. You know, give me some tips on my swing?"

Rage shakes his head hard. "Please, man, don't. I'll do whatever you want."

I chuckle. "It's funny you say that. I think your buddy Jet would've said the same if I'd given him a chance. Unfortunately, it's hard to speak when your guts are getting carved out."

Rage's eyes widen. "You're the one who took out Jet? That was you? You piece of shit!"

I laugh again.

"What's so funny, you sick bastard?"

"What's funny is that I'm about to paint this room with your brain, and you're actually shocked I'm capable of killing your freak friend. And, Rage, as far as being a sick

219

bastard goes, you hold the trophy for that. Anyone capable of drugging and raping young girls isn't just sick—they're demented. And do you know what they used to do to demented patients years ago?"

Rage's face fills with fear as he shakes his head.

I swing the club over my shoulder and crouch in front of him. "First, they'd perform an exorcism. If that didn't work, they'd shove a knife in the person's brain and sever the neutral connectors that control things like memory, function, and guess what else?"

Rage's eyes fixate on me. He doesn't answer.

"That's okay. I didn't think you'd know the answer." I stand up and run my hand up and down the shaft of the iron. "The last reason they performed a lobotomy was to control emotions. But you don't have to worry about that. You clearly don't have a shred of remorse or shame for what you've done."

He finally manages to speak. "I do."

"Oh. Really? If that's true, tell me my sister's name."

Rage looks at me with desperation.

"I want to hear you say it!"

"I...I...uh—"

"Nothing's coming to you?" I tilt my head. "That doesn't sound like remorse to me."

"Come on, man. I met a lot of girls. How the hell am I supposed to remember all their names?"

As I stare at the weasel, shaking, whimpering, and begging, I picture my fair-haired, innocent sister. How much love and joy she had. She could have done amazing things with her life. But the slimy little waste of skin cowering in the corner hurt her so badly that he killed her soul, leaving only a dark echo of who she used to be.

My eyes burn, and my chest tightens. "Her name was Hannah, you sick fuck."

My first swing connects with the precision of a golf pro. Again and again, I swing the club, never losing my momentum.

With pieces of brain, bone, and tissue on both sides of the corner wall, I eventually drop my arm, then stand back to admire my efforts. "Not bad. Not bad at all. Maybe I should take up golf."

For a brief moment, I feel like I've bested the devil. That is until I hear the lingering moans.

"Oh, that's right." I turn to look at the other man on the floor. "There's still you."

Raven looks up at me, eyes wide with fear as he grips his blood-soaked leg. "Lance—no hard feelings, man. I'm pretty fucked up here. I can't stop the bleeding. You got me good. I think we're even."

"Gee, Raven, I don't know. I just spent all that time getting warmed up on Rage. I'd hate to waste this adrenaline."

He tries to smile at me. "I think it's great you got rid of Rage. He was a tyrant. He made all of us do things we didn't want to do. I'm glad he's gone. I should thank you."

I laugh. "You should thank me? Is that what you were doing when you cracked my skull with a heavy piece of iron?" I hold up the club.

Suddenly, the girl cries out from the bed, her voice dopey. "Help me."

I walk over and pull the blanket over her. "It's okay. I'm going to get you out of here. I'll be right back."

My stomach twists as I think about what could have happened to this young girl. A wave of pain and dizziness hits me when I turn back and look down at Raven. His face is now chalky as he grips his leg and breaths hard.

"Not feeling too good, huh? Yeah. I can relate. But I think I have it all figured out."

"You do?" His tone is weary.

"Absolutely. Let me explain." I point at him with the club. "Your actions have put you in this shitty situation. It's cause and effect. You get it?"

He stares at me with hollow eyes, oblivious to the meaning of my words.

"Okay, you're struggling with the whole processing thing. Let me simplify. You decided to participate in a gang rape of my sister, which eventually claimed her life. That means you have a debt to pay. An eye for an eye. Does that clear things up for you?"

"I swear, man, if you let me go, I'll call the cops on myself. Just please don't hurt me—"

"Say that last part again." I hold a hand up to my bloody ear.

"Please don't hurt me."

"I bet that's exactly what my baby sister said while she was drugged and repeatedly violated by all four of you worthless pieces of shit."

I grip the golf club firmly, then sit on Raven's long, boney body. He puts his bloody hands up. "I'm sorry, man, I'm so sorry. Don't do this—"

I force his arms aside, lay the bar of the club across his throat, and push down. He scratches and claws at my forearms, making a bloody mess of my skin, but I only push harder, putting the full weight of my body into it. I watch him flail and change colour, kicking his legs and twisting his body, but I don't ease up.

It doesn't take as long as I thought it would to kill the little pig. Or maybe I enjoyed it so much, the time passed quickly. Either way, once I'm satisfied that he's dead, I climb off and throw the club in the corner, on top of Rage or what's left of him.

The girl moans again, then whispers, "I want to go home."

I walk over to the bed, picking up the long white skirt from the floor on the way. I remove the blanket and gently put the skirt on her. I then pull down her top so she's covered and carefully help her sit up. She pukes immediately, covering us both in a yellow bile, likely containing whatever drug they gave her.

"I'm sorry." Her voice is soft and weak.

"It's okay, girl. Throw up all you can. Do you think you can walk if I help you?"

She shakes her head. "I don't think so, but I'll try."

I grab her hands and pull her to her feet. Her legs have no strength, and she falls to the floor. I take a deep breath, then crouch down. I lift and cradle her in my arms, just about blacking out.

Slowly, I turn toward the door, then walk. All the adrenaline I had quickly fades, and the pain returns to my head with a vengeance.

The walk down the long, black hallway and through the front room to the door seems to take forever. When I finally reach out to turn the handle, my vision blurs, giving me vertigo. I lose sight of the handle, and my body teeters.

Again, I try sliding my hand across the door until my fingers feel the knob. I slowly turn it, keeping a firm hold on the girl. Then, suddenly, the knob turns on its own, the door swings open, and I stumble backward.

"What the fuck is going on?"

I strain to focus as Blacky stares at me from the doorway, a brown bag in his hand.

"Where the hell is Raven and Rage?" he demands.

I fight to stay standing. "In the back room. Dead. I've got a gun in my pocket, and unless you turn around and get the hell out of here, you're next."

I want him badly. But I know my consciousness is fading. If I try to take him down in my weakened state, I might lose, and the girl in my arms will be at his mercy. I can't take that chance.

Blacky is frozen on the stoop. I can only imagine what I must look like, with thick blood trails running from my head, covering my ears and neck, and chunks of flesh gouged off my forearms from Raven's fight to survive.

Blacky shakes his head, wide-eyed. "This is fucked up, man." Then, he backs away from the door and walks sideways down the stairs, keeping his eyes on me the whole time. Just like that, he disappears into the darkness. I hope to hell I see him again.

I stumble to the top of the stairs, my body swaying. Knowing I have nothing more to fight with and not an ounce of strength remaining, I take one step down and sit hard on the stair.

I look at the girl curled up like a child in my arms. I can hear her breathe like she's in a deep, safe sleep. I gently kiss her forehead and rock slowly, back and forth.

I couldn't save you, Hannah, and I'm so sorry. But the monsters are gone now. Well, most of them. And they can't hurt anyone anymore. That wouldn't have been possible if you hadn't gone through what you did.

A foreign feeling, like pressure, pushes against my eyes. Then I feel the salty moisture sting my face.

* * *

The annoying beeps hurt my ears. I fight my way through the exhaustion to reach over and shut off the alarm, but my arm can only go so far before it stops. *What the hell is going on?*

My eyelids feel sticky and heavy as I strain to open them. The first thing I see is a lot of white, white walls, a white ceiling, and a white floor. *This isn't my bedroom.*

I slowly turn my head to find the source of the insistent beeping. That's when I notice tubes and wires hooked to my arms, and my wrists tied to the curved metal bars of a bed. *I'm in a hospital. Why the hell am I here?*

My heart pounds as a wave of anxiety rushes through me. I don't remember coming to the hospital. I try to yell, but only a whisper escapes.

An authoritative voice speaks. "Calm down. You're okay."

I turn to face the white curtain beside me, and a hand emerges and pulls the drape back. A man about forty is sitting in a chair no more than five feet from the edge of the bed.

"What's going on? What am I doing here?"

"I'm Officer Swanson, and you're in the hospital. Calm down."

"But what's wrong with me?"

"You don't remember?"

I shake my head slowly. "No. I haven't got a bloody clue."

No sooner do the words leave my lips than I picture the young girl in my arms. With that, I lie quietly for a moment and close my eyes.

Slowly, memories seep back of going to USH's band house and walking down the black hallway. The girl on the bed, half-naked, with Rage hovering over her.

The following images that flash through my mind are of me lying on the floor. I recall most of what had occurred, piece by piece, image by image.

I open my eyes and focus on the cop. "What happened to the girl? Is she okay?"

He nods. "Regardless of the brutal way you murdered the two men in the house, you did a good thing by rescuing her."

I breathe a huge sigh of relief, knowing the girl is safe. Then I think about my own hide. "They were really bad people. And I never went to their place with the intention to kill anyone."

"Save your strength. We'll get a statement from you later. Just relax until the doctor comes back."

"How long have I been here?"

"Four days."

"What?" Again, my heart rate accelerates. "I've been out cold for that long?"

I wonder what my injuries are. I remember getting the golf club to the head and hearing a crack. I just hope I don't have a brain injury.

As my mind reels, it takes an unbearably long time before the doctor walks in. When he finally does, he's a young guy carrying a clipboard and speaking with a soft, low tone. He tells me that I have a fractured skull and a bad concussion. He assures me I am lucky, though I don't really feel like I am after hearing the news.

When he leaves the room, Officer Swanson gets up and follows him. A few minutes later, the officer returns, saying there's a family member here to visit. I scoff and am about to explain that none of my family is living when I see Reg's face peering through the glass on the door. I swallow my words. "Great. Thank you. I could really use seeing a family member right now."

The officer waves to Reg, signaling him to enter.

Reg looks at me with horror, then tries to downplay his reaction. "Hey, cousin. How are you feeling?"

"I feel great. Just got back from the weight room, and they're going to install a stripper pole in here so I can work on my upper body strength."

Reg shakes his head. "Just as much of a smart-ass as always. A good sign." He walks over to the bedside and sits in a chair. "Well, I guess things kind of spun out of control, hey, Lance?"

"Fair statement. I think I'm kind of fucked now."

"At least you're going to be okay. I spoke with the doctor in the hallway. He said with a lot of rest, you'll heal."

"Yeah, but my life will never be the same after getting busted."

Reg nods slowly. "I got a call the night you were found at the band house. They ran the bike plates and got all my information from there."

"Oh yeah, the bike. Did you pick it up from there?"

"No. I couldn't. They kept it for evidence."

"Why?"

"I don't know, man. Something about tire tracks and blood. They haven't divulged much more about it yet."

"I'm sorry you got involved in all of this. You've been such a good friend over the years." Realizing what I said, I glance over at the cop. "I mean, cousin."

"I guess it'll be a while before we can go to another concert together."

"Yeah. Where I'm going, I don't think they'll give me a pass to attend a rock concert soon."

Reg leans in close. "I can't believe I'm saying this, considering my views on violence, but thanks for doing what you did. Once the full story hits the media, I don't think many will shed a tear over those deviants."

I smile. "You know what's weird? I only went to that house to retrieve Hannah's necklace and some other shit they had of mine. I'd lost all that violent energy I'd felt for so long. But I couldn't just walk away when I saw the girl on the bed. I had to do something."

"I get it, Lance. Many others will too."

Officer Swanson clears his throat. "Okay, guys. Times up."

Reg is slow to stand. He reaches over and squeezes my hand. "Whenever I can, I will be here or wherever you go next."

As soon as Reg leaves, the officer looks at me. "That Reg is a solid friend. You're lucky to have someone willing to stand by you, considering the hot water you're in."

"My cousin? Yeah, he's great."

"Let it go, Lance. I'm fully aware he's not related to you."

"Then why did you let him in?"

He gives me a long look. "Let's just say I've got two teenage daughters that like to go to concerts."

"Thanks, man. I appreciate it."

Epilogue

When I hear the key in the door, I put down my book and sit on the cot.

A barrel-chested guard jingles a heavy set of keys. "You've got a visitor."

Walking in front of him down the shiny beige hall, I think about the studio in Zurich. If things had gone according to plan with me leaving, I'd be sitting in the control room, laying down tracks right now.

Then, as one of the other inmates passes us, he gives me a nod and a smile—a sign of respect. At that moment, I remember that although losing my freedom was a hefty price, I have peace of mind knowing I saved a young girl, and probably many others, from suffering the same fate as Hannah.

The guard leads me through a heavy grey door, then points to a row of booths in the middle of the floor. He tells me which one to sit at, then leans against the wall and watches me.

I sit down and gaze at the sunlight streaming through the long, narrow windows, and I remember the smell of the salt air. In this cement jungle, there is only dank, heavy air—no breeze, no scents from nature.

A few minutes later, I hear a door open at the other end of the large room, then footsteps getting louder. I grin when I see Reg on the other side of the plexiglass. As soon as he sits down, I pick up my phone and motion him to do the same.

"You look good, Reg. You must've found a lady friend to show you how to do your laundry."

He shakes his head. "No such luck. Not after the shit you went through. I'll concede to being a bachelor for the rest of my life."

"Nah. Don't be crazy. You'll change your mind once you meet the right one. Plus, one of us has to be getting some. I'll have to live vicariously through you, so don't stay celibate too long."

There's a brief pause. Then the corners of Reg's mouth drop. "I wished like hell that none of this happened."

"I don't. I'm glad I did what I did. I wouldn't change a thing, except for maybe the getting caught part." I chuckle.

"It's too bad you couldn't have gotten a lesser sentence on a temporary insanity plea."

"Wouldn't have worked. They knew I wasn't nuts, just really pissed off." I let out a sigh. "It's not surprising I got the book thrown at me. The prosecution had a heavy hitter like Perry Mason, and I had Mr. Bean. As soon as the trial began, I knew I was sunk.

And I wouldn't doubt it if Jet's father influenced the judge."

Reg nods sadly. "So, is it horrible in here?"

"Well, it's no cakewalk. But it's not as bad as the movies portray it, either. Most of the other inmates respect me for getting rid of rapists, so I don't have to carve a shank to protect myself. Other than having to shower with my pants on, it's not so bad."

Reg's eyes widen. "Fuck, dude. Are you serious? You have to shower in your clothes?"

I laugh. "That's what I love about you, Reg. It's always been so easy to yank your chain."

"You're an asshole." He chuckles. "Remember when we saw River Dogs in L.A.?"

"Yeah, that was insane. Great concert great night. And to think we almost couldn't go because of those bogus tickets you bought. What did you pay for them again?"

Reg's voice is low. "Five hundred."

I laugh. "I hope they kissed you before they screwed you."

"Nope. Didn't even get a handshake."

"Good thing I met that legit guy in front of the stadium. And I only paid a couple hundred bucks for both tickets."

"You're never going to stop ribbing me about that, are you?"

"Nope."

Reg quickly changes the subject. "Hey, guess what? When the story about you and USH came out online, thousands of people were in the comments, including reputable musicians. You're like royalty."

"What did they say?

"That they support your actions, even if they were brutal. They love that you saved that girl, no matter what you did to accomplish it."

"Good. The next time you come, write down which musicians left messages. I'll get a kick out of it."

He nods, then changes the subject to music without warning in true Reg fashion. "What about Cross Country Driver? Have you seen their new videos yet?"

"Look around, Reg. I'm in jail. It's not like I have unlimited access to a computer."

"Too bad, man. 'So Fly' is out of this world. Rob Lamothe's voice is accompanied by world-renowned musicians, so there's no way it could be anything less than what it is—excellent!"

"That doesn't surprise me. Whenever I heard Lamothe, no matter what project he was working on, his voice tripped me out. I never understood how he could emit such feel and soul on some songs and then, with the same conviction, rock the fuck out on others." I shake my head. "I don't think there's a style of music out there that he couldn't conquer."

Just as the guard pushes off the wall and heads in my direction, indicating that it's time I returned to my cell, Reg says, "I've got a bit of news that might make your day."

"What's that? You're going to break my ass out of here and take me to a killer concert?"

He shakes his head. "Unfortunately not. But check this out. The last living member of USH, Blacky, the guy you didn't take out, met his maker last night."

"What do you mean?"

"It turns out he was at Lulu's, bragging about how he confronted you. A while after, he left the bar alone, and someone drove into him. Splashed him all over the outside of the bar."

"That's crazy. Do they know who did it?"

Reg smiles. "Nope. But an eyewitness thought she saw an older mode compact car leaving the scene."

I smile. *Jenny. Good job, girl.*

When the guard touches my shoulder, I nod to Reg and tell him to return soon. Then I stand up with my shoulders back and walk proudly toward the heavy metal doors.

In my room, I lie on my bunk and stare at the ceiling, feeling complete harmony with everything that's happened and where I am.

"Hey, man. Is everything cool?" my cellmate, Roger, who's doing ten years for arson, asks.

"Yeah, I'm cool. Never better."

"If you want, I can give you that tattoo on your arm we talked about."

"Sure, why not."

A few hours later, I look down at the bleeding, scabbing mess on my arm and see the faint outline of a rat, the word *"Exterminator"* written above it.

The End

If you enjoyed this book, please leave the author a review.

2022 Bestselling Author
Jay Lang

Jay Lang grew up on the ocean, splitting her time between Read Island and Vancouver Island before moving to Vancouver to work as a TV, film and commercial actress. Eventually she left the industry for a quieter life on a live-a-board boat, where she worked as a clothing designer for rock bands. Five years later she moved to Abbotsford to attend university. There, she fell in love with creative writing and wrote five novel manuscripts in a year. She spends her days hiking and drawing inspiration for her writing from nature.

BWL Publishing

bwlpublishing.ca